Prelude in
the House of the Dead

The man walks through his Thousandyear Eve in the House of the Dead. If you could look about the enormous room through which he walks, you couldn't see a thing. It is far too dark for eyes to be of value.

For this dark time, we'll simply refer to him as "the man."

There are two reasons for doing so:

First, he fits the general and generally accepted description of an unmodified, male, human-model being—walking upright, having opposable thumbs and possessing the other typical characteristics of the profession; and second, because his name has been taken from him.

There is no reason to be more specific at this point.

In his right hand, the man bears the staff of his Master, and it guides him through the dark. It tugs him this way, that way. It burns his hand, his fingers, his opposing thumb if his foot strays a step from its ordained path.

When the man reaches a certain place within the darkness,

he mounts seven steps to a stone dais and raps three times upon it with the staff.

Then there is light, dim and orange and crowded into corners. It shows the edges of the enormous, unfilled room.

He reverses the staff and screws it into a socket in the stone.

Had you ears in that room, you would hear a sound as of winged insects circling near you, withdrawing, returning.

Only the man hears it, though. There are over two thousand other people present, but they are all of them dead.

They come up out of the transparent rectangles which now appear in the floor, come up unbreathing, unblinking and horizontal, and they rest upon invisible catafalques at a height of two feet, and their garments and their skins are of all colors and their bodies of all ages. Now some have wings and some have tails, and some have horns and some long talons. Some have all of these things, and some have pieces of machinery built into them and some do not. Many others look like the man, unmodified.

The man wears yellow breeches and a sleeveless shirt of the same color. His belt and cloak are black. He stands beside his Master's gleaming staff, and he regards the dead beneath him.

"Get up!" he calls out. "All of you!"

And his words mix with the humming that is in the air and are repeated over and over and again, not like an echo, fading, but persistent and recurring, with the force of an electric alarm.

The air is filled and stirred. There comes a moaning and a creaking of brittle joints, then movement.

Rustling, clicking, chafing, they sit up, they stand up.

Then sound and movement cease, and the dead stand like unlit candles beside their opened graves.

The man climbs down from the dais, stands a moment before it, then says, "Follow me!" and he walks back the way he came, leaving his Master's staff vibrating in the gray air.

As he walks, he comes to a woman who is tall and golden

Creatures of Light and Darkness

Creatures of
Light and
Darkness

ROGER ZELAZNY

An Imprint of HarperCollinsPublishers

This book was originally published in 1969 by Doubleday & Company, Inc. It was reprinted by arrangement with Doubleday in a paperback edition in 1970 by Avon Books, an imprint of HarperCollins Publishers.

Portions of this book appeared in *New Worlds* and *If* magazine, copyright © 1968, 1969 by Galaxy Publishing Corporation.

First Eos trade paperback edition published 2010.

Eos is a federally registered trademark of HarperCollins Publishers.

Designed by Paula Russell Szafranski

The Library of Congress has cataloged the original hardcover edition as follows:

Zelazny, Roger.
  Creatures of light and darkness / Roger Zelazny.— 1st ed.
    p. cm.
  ISBN-10: 0-380-01122-0
  PZ4.Z456 Cr PS3576.E43
  813'.5'4

70078673

ISBN 978-0-06-193645-6 (pbk.)

10 11 12 13 14 WBC/RRD 10 9 8 7 6 5 4 3 2 1

To Chip Delany, Just Because

Generations pass away and others go on,
since the time of the ancestors.
They that build buildings,
their places are no more.
What has been done with them?

I have heard the words of Imhotep and Hardedef,
with whose sayings men speak so much.
What are their places now?

Their walls are crumbled,
their places are non-existent,
as if they had never been.

No one returns from there,
so that he might tell us their disposition,
that he might tell us how they are,
that he might still our hearts
until we shall go to the place where they have gone.

Make holiday and weary not therein!
Behold, it is not given to a man
to take his property with him.
Behold, no one who goes can come back again.

—HARRIS 500, 6:2–9.

Comus *enters with a Charming Rod in one hand, his Glass in
the other; with him a rout of Monsters, headed like sundry sorts
of wild Beasts. They come in making a riotous and unruly noise,
with Torches in their hands.*

—MILTON.

The Human Dress is forged with Iron,
The Human Form is a fiery Forge,
The Human Face a Furnace seal'd,
The Human Heart is a hungry Gorge.

—BLAKE.

and a suicide: He stares into her unseeing eyes and says, "Do you know me?" and the orange lips, the dead lips, the dry lips move, and they whisper, "No," but he stares longer and says, "*Did* you know me?" and the air hums with his words, until she says, "No," once again, and he passes her by.

He questions two others: a man who had been ancient of days, with a clock built into his left wrist, and a black dwarf with horns and hooves and the tail of a goat. But both say, "No," and they fall into step behind him, and they follow him out of that enormous room and into another, where more lie under stone, not really waiting, to be called forth for his Thousandyear Eve in the House of the Dead.

The man leads them. He leads the dead whom he has summoned back to movement, and they follow him. They follow him through corridors and galleries and halls, and up wide, straight stairways and down narrow, winding stairways, and they come at last into the great Hall of the House of the Dead, where his Master holds his court.

He sits on a black throne of polished stone, and there are metal bowls of fire to his right and to his left. On each of the two hundred pillars that line his high Hall, a torch blazes and flickers and its spark-shot smoke coils and puffs upward, becoming at last a gray part of the flowing cloud that covers the ceiling completely.

He does not move, but he regards the man as he advances across the Hall, five thousand of the dead at his back, and his eyes lay red upon him as he comes forward.

The man prostrates himself at his feet, and he does not move until he is addressed:

"You may greet me and rise," come the words, each of them a sharp, throaty stab in the midst of an audible exhalation.

"Hail, Anubis, Master of the House of the Dead!" says the man, and he stands.

Anubis lowers his black muzzle slightly and his fangs are white within it. Red lightning, his tongue, darts forward, re-enters his mouth. He stands then, and the shadows slide downward upon his bare and man-formed body.

He raises his left hand and the humming sound comes into the Hall, and it carries his words through the flickering light and the smoke:

"You who are dead," he says, "tonight you will disport yourselves for my pleasure. Food and wine will pass between your dead lips, though you will not taste it. Your dead stomachs will hold it within you, while your dead feet take the measure of a dance. Your dead mouths will speak words that will have no meaning to you, and you will embrace one another without pleasure. You will sing for me if I wish it. You will lie down again when I will it."

He raises his right hand.

"Let the revelry begin," he says, and he claps his hands together.

Then tables slide forward from between the pillars, laden with food and with drink, and there is music upon the air.

The dead move to obey him.

"You may join them," Anubis says to the man, and he re-seats himself upon his throne.

The man crosses to the nearest table and eats lightly and drinks a glass of wine. The dead dance about him, but he does not dance with them. They make noises which are words without meaning, and he does not listen to them. He pours a second glass of wine and the eyes of Anubis are upon him as he drinks it. He pours a third glass and he holds it in his hands and sips at it and stares into it.

How much time has passed he cannot tell, when Anubis says, "Servant!"

He stands, turns.

"Approach!" says Anubis, and he does so.

4

"You may rise. You know what night tonight is?"

"Yes, Master. It is Thousandyear Eve."

"It is *your* Thousandyear Eve. This night we celebrate an anniversary. You have served me for a full thousand years in the House of the Dead. Are you glad?"

"Yes, Master . . ."

"You recall my promise?"

"Yes. You told me that if I served you faithfully for a thousand years, then you would give me back my name. You would tell me who I had been in the Middle Worlds of Life."

"I beg your pardon, but I did not."

"You . . . ?"

"I told you that I would give you *a* name, which is a different thing altogether."

"But I thought . . ."

"I do not care what you thought. Do you want a name?"

"Yes, Master . . ."

". . . But you would prefer your old one? Is that what you are trying to say?"

"Yes."

"Do you really think that anyone would remember your name after ten centuries? Do you think that you were so important in the Middle Worlds that someone would have noted down your name, that it would have mattered to anyone?"

"I do not know."

"But you want it back?"

"If I may have it, Master."

"Why? Why do you want it?"

"Because I remember nothing of the Worlds of Life. I would like to know who I was when I dwelled there."

"Why? For what purpose?"

"I cannot answer you, because I do not know."

"Of all the dead," says Anubis, "you know that I have brought only you back to full consciousness to serve me here. Do you feel this means that perhaps there is something special about you?"

"I have often wondered why you did as you did."

"Then let me give you ease, man: You are nothing. You were nothing. You are not remembered. Your mortal name does not signify anything."

The man lowers his eyes.

"Do you doubt me?"

"No, Master . . ."

"Why not?"

"Because you do not lie."

"Then let me show it. I took away your memories of life only because they would give you pain among the dead. But now let me demonstrate your anonymity. There are over five thousand of the dead in this room, from many ages and places."

Anubis stands, and his voice carries to every presence in the Hall:

"Attend me, maggots! Turn your eyes toward this man who stands before my throne! —Face them, man!"

The man turns about.

"Man, know that today you do not wear the body you slept in last night. You look now as you did a thousand years ago, when you came into the House of the Dead."

"My dead ones, are there any of you here present who can look upon this man and say that you know him?"

A golden girl steps forward.

"I know this man," she says, through orange lips, "because he spoke to me in the other hall."

"That I know," says Anubis, "but who is he?"

"He is the one who spoke to me."

"That is no answer. Go and copulate with yon purple lizard. —And what of you, old man?"

"He spoke to me also."

"That I know. Can you name him?"

6

"I cannot."

"Then go dance on yonder table and pour wine over your head. —What of you, black man?"

"This man also spoke with me."

"Do you know his name?"

"I did not know it when he asked me—"

"Then burn!" cries Anubis, and fires fall down from the ceiling and leap out from the walls and crisp the black man to ashes, which move then in slow eddies across the floor, passing among the ankles of the stopped dancers, falling finally into final dust.

"You see?" says Anubis. "There is none to name you as once you were known."

"I see," says the man, "but the last might have had further words—"

"To waste! You are unknown and unwanted, save by me. This, because you are fairly adept at the various embalming arts and you occasionally compose a clever epitaph."

"Thank you, Master."

"What good would a name and memories do you here?"

"None, I suppose."

"Yet you wish a name, so I shall give you one. Draw your dagger."

The man draws the blade which hangs at his left side.

"Now cut off your thumb."

"Which thumb, Master?"

"The left one will do."

The man bites his lower lip and tightens his eyes as he drags the blade against the joint of his thumb. His blood falls upon the floor. It runs along the blade of the knife and trickles from its point. He drops to his knees and continues to cut, tears streaming down his cheeks and falling to mingle with the blood. His breath comes in gasps and a single sob escapes him.

Then, "It is done," he says. "Here!" He drops the blade and offers Anubis his thumb.

"I don't want the thing! Throw it into the flames!"

With his right hand, the man throws his thumb into a brazier. It sputters, sizzles, flares.

"Now cup your left hand and collect the blood within it."

The man does this thing.

"Now raise it above your head and let it drip down upon you."

He raises his hand and the blood falls onto his forehead.

"Now repeat after me: 'I baptize me . . .'"

"'I baptize me . . .'"

"'Wakim, of the House of the Dead . . .'"

"'Wakim, of the House of the Dead . . .'"

"'In the name of Anubis . . .'"

"'In the name of Anubis . . .'"

"'Wakim . . .'"

"'Wakim . . .'"

"'Emissary of Anubis in the Middle Worlds . . .'"

"'Emissary of Anubis in the Middle Worlds . . .'"

"'. . . and beyond.'"

"'. . . and beyond.'"

"Hear me now, oh you dead ones: I proclaim this man Wakim. Repeat his name!"

"*Wakim*," comes the word, through dead lips.

"So be it! You are named now, Wakim," he says. "It is fitting, therefore, that you feel your birth into namehood, that you come away changed by this thing, oh my named one!"

Anubis raises both hands about his head and lowers them to his sides.

"Resume dancing!" he commands the dead.

They move to the music once more.

The body-cutting machine rolls into the hall, and the prosthetic replacement machine follows it.

Wakim looks away from them, but they draw up beside him and stop.

The first machine extrudes restrainers and holds him.

"Human arms are weak," says Anubis. "Let these be removed."

The man screams as the saw blades hum. Then he passes out. The dead continue their dance.

When Wakim awakens, two seamless silver arms hang at his sides, cold and insensitive. He flexes the fingers.

"And human legs be slow, and capable of fatigue. Let those he wears be exchanged for tireless metal."

When Wakim awakens the second time, he stands upon silver pillars. He wiggles his toes. Anubis' tongue darts forth.

"Place your right hand into the flames," he says, "and hold it there until it glows white."

The music falls around him, and the flames caress his hand until it matches their red. The dead talk their dead talk and drink the wine they do not taste. They embrace one another without pleasure. The hand glows white.

"Now," says Anubis, "seize your manhood in your right hand and burn it away."

Wakim licks his lips.

"Master . . ." he says.

"Do it!"

He does this thing, and he falls to unconsciousness before he has finished.

When he awakens again and looks down upon himself, he is all of gleaming silver, sexless and strong. When he touches his forehead, there comes the sound of metal upon metal.

"How do you feel, Wakim?" asks Anubis.

"I do not know," he answers, and his voice comes strange and harsh.

Anubis gestures, and the nearest side of the cutting machine becomes a reflecting surface.

"Regard yourself."

Wakim stares at the shining egg that is his head, at the yellow lenses, his eyes, the gleaming barrel, his chest.

"Men may begin and end in many ways," says Anubis. "Some may start as machines and gain their humanity slowly. Others may end as machines, losing humanity by pieces as they live. That which is lost may always be regained. That which is gained may always be lost. —What are you, Wakim, a man or a machine?"

"I do not know."

"Then let me confuse you further."

Anubis gestures, and Wakim's arms and legs come loose, fall away. His metal torso clangs against stone, rolls, then lies at the foot of the throne.

"Now you lack mobility," says Anubis.

He reaches forward with his foot and touches a tiny switch at the back of Wakim's head.

"Now you lack all senses but hearing."

"Yes," answers Wakim.

"Now a connection is being attached to you. You feel nothing, but your head is opened and you are about to become a part of the machine which monitors and maintains this entire world. See it all now!"

"I do," he replies, as he becomes conscious of every room, corridor, hall and chamber in the always dead never alive world that has never been a world, a world made, not begotten of coalesced starstuff and the fires of creation, but hammered and jointed, riveted and fused, insulated and decorated, not into seas and land and air, and life, but oils and metals and stone and walls of energy, all hung together within the icy void where no sun shines; and he is aware of distances, stresses, weights, materials, pressures and the secret numbers of the dead. He is not aware of his body, mechanical and disconnected. He knows only the waves of maintenance movement that flow through the House of the Dead. He flows with them and he knows the colorless colors of quantity perception.

Then Anubis speaks again:

"You know every shadow in the House of the Dead. You have looked through all the hidden eyes."

"Yes."

"Now see what lies beyond."

There are stars, stars, scattered stars, blackness all between. They ripple and fold and bend, and they rush toward him, rush by him. Their colors are blazing and pure as angels' eyes, and they pass near, pass far, in the eternity through which he seems to move. There is no sense of real time or real movement, only a changing of the field. A great blue Tophet Box of a sun seems to soar beside him for a moment, and then again comes black, all about him, and more small lights that pass, distantly.

And he comes at last to a world that is not a world, citrine and azure and green, green, green. A green corona hangs about it, at thrice its own diameter, and it seems to pulsate with a pleasant rhythm.

"Behold the House of Life," says Anubis, from somewhere.

And he does. It is warm and glowing and alive. He has a feeling of aliveness.

"Osiris rules the House of Life," says Anubis.

And he beholds a great bird-head atop human shoulders, bright yellow eyes within it, alive, alive-oh; and the creature stands before him on an endless plain of living green which is superimposed upon his view of the world, and he holds the Staff of Life in his one hand and the Book of Life in his other. He seems to be the source of the radiant warmth.

Wakim then hears the voice of Anubis again:

"The House of Life and the House of the Dead contain the Middle Worlds."

And there is a falling, swirling sensation, and Wakim looks upon stars once more, but stars separated and held from other stars by bonds of force that are visible, then invisible, then visible again, fading, coming, going, white, glowing lines, fluctuating.

"You now perceive the Middle Worlds of Life," says Anubis.

11

And dozens of worlds roll before him like balls of exotic marble, stippled, gauged, polished, incadescent.

". . . Contained," says Anubis. "They are contained within the field which arcs between the only two poles that matter."

"Poles?" says the metal head that is Wakim.

"The House of Life and the House of the Dead. The Middle Worlds about their suns do move, and all together go on the paths of Life and Death."

"I do not understand," says Wakim.

"Of course you do not understand. What is at the same time the greatest blessing and the greatest curse in the universe?"

"I do not know."

"Life," says Anubis, "or death."

"I do not understand," says Wakim. "You used the superlative. You called for one answer. You named two things, however."

"Did I?" asks Anubis. "Really? Just because I used two words, does it mean that I have named two separate and distinct things? May a thing not have more than one name? Take yourself for an example. What are you?"

"I do not know."

"That may be the beginning of wisdom, then. You could as easily be a machine which I chose to incarnate as a man for a time and have now returned to a metal casing, as you could be a man whom I have chosen to incarnate as a machine."

"Then what difference does it make?"

"None. None whatsoever. But you cannot make the distinction. You cannot remember. Tell me, are you alive?"

"Yes."

"Why?"

"I think. I hear your voice. I have memories. I can speak."

"Which of these qualities is life? Remember that you do not breathe, your nervous system is a mass of metallic strands and I have burnt your heart. Remember, too, that I have machines that can outreason you, outremember you, outtalk you. What does that leave you with as an excuse for saying you are alive? You say that you hear my voice, and 'hearing' is a subjective phenomenon? Very well. I shall disconnect your hearing also. Watch closely to see whether you cease to exist."

. . . One snowflake drifting down a well, a well without waters, without walls, without bottom, without top. Now take away the snowflake and consider the drifting. . . .

After a timeless time, Anubis' voice comes once again:

"Do you know the difference between life and death?"

" 'I' am life," says Wakim. "Whatever you give or take away, if 'I' remain it is life."

"Sleep," says Anubis, and there is nothing to hear him, there in the House of the Dead.

When Wakim awakens, he finds that he has been set upon a table near to the throne, and he can see once more, and he regards the dance of the dead and he hears the music to which they move.

"Were you dead?" asks Anubis.

"No," says Wakim. "I was sleeping."

"What is the difference?"

" 'I' was still there, although I did not know it."

Anubis laughs.

"Suppose I had never awakened you?"

"That, I suppose, would be death."

"Death? If I did not choose to exercise my power to awaken you? Even though the power was ever present, and 'you' potential and available for that same ever?"

"If this thing were not done, if I remained forever only potential, then this would be death."

"A moment ago you said that sleep and death were two different things. Is it that the period of time involved makes a difference?"

"No," says Wakin, "it is a matter of existence. After sleep there

13

comes wakefulness, and the life is still present. When I exist, I know it. When I do not, I know nothing."

"Life, then, is nothing?"

"No."

"Life, then, is existing? Like these dead?"

"No," says Wakim. "It is knowing you exist, at least some of the time."

"Of what is this a process?"

" 'I,' " says Wakim.

"And what is 'I'? Who are you?"

"I am Wakim."

"I only named you a short while ago! What were you before that?"

"Not Wakim."

"Dead?"

"No! Alive!" cries Wakim.

"Do not raise you voice within my halls," says Anubis. "You do not know what you are or who you are, you do not know the difference between existing and not existing, yet you presume to argue with me concerning life and death! Now I shall not ask you, I shall tell you. I shall tell you of life and of death.

"There is too much life and there is not enough life," he begins, "and the same goes for death. Now I shall throw away paradoxes.

"The House of Life lies so far from here that a ray of light which left it on the day you entered this domain would not yet have traveled a significant fraction of the distance which separates us. Between us lie the Middle Worlds. They move within the Life-Death tides that flow between my House and the House of Osiris. When I say 'flow' I do not mean that they move like that pitiful ray of light, crawling. Rather, they move like waves on the ocean which has but two shores. We may raise waves anywhere we wish without disrupting the entire sea. What are these waves, and what do they do?

14

"Some worlds have too much life," he says. "Life—crawling, pullulating, fecundating, smothering itself—worlds too clement, too full of the sciences which keep men alive—worlds which would drown themselves in their own semen, worlds which would pack all of their lands with crowds of big-bellied women— and so go down to death beneath the weight of their own fruitfulness. Then there are worlds which are bleak and barren and bitter, worlds which grind life like grain. Even with body modifications and with world-change machines, there are only a few hundred worlds which may be inhabited by the six intelligent races. Life is needed badly in the worst of these. It can be a deadly blessing on the best. When I say that life is needed or not needed in certain places, I am of course also saying that death is needed or not needed. I am not speaking of two different things, but of the same thing. Osiris and I are bookkeepers. We credit and we debit. We raise waves, or we cause waves to sink back again into the ocean. Can life be counted upon to limit itself? No. It is the mindless striving of two to become infinity. Can death be counted upon to limit itself? Never. It is the equally mindless effort of zero to encompass infinity.

"But there must be life control and death control," he says, "else the fruitful worlds would rise and fall, rise and fall, cycling between empire and anarchy, then down to final disruption. The bleak worlds would be encompassed by zero. Life cannot contain itself within the bounds statistics have laid down for its guidance. Therefore, it must be contained, and it is. Osiris and I hold the Middle Worlds. They lie within our field of control, and we turn them on and we turn them off as we would. Do you see now, Wakim? Do you begin to understand?"

"You limit life? You cause death?"

"We can lay sterility on any or all of the six races on any world we choose, for as long a period of time as is necessary. This can be done on an absolute or a fractional basis. We may also manipulate life spans, decimate populations."

"How?"

"Fire. Famine. Plague. War."

"What of the sterile worlds, the dry worlds? What of those?"

"Multiple births can be insured, and we do not tamper with life spans. The newly dead are sent to the House of Life, not here. There they are repaired, or their parts used in the construction of new individuals, who may or may not host a human mentality."

"And of the other dead?"

"The House of the Dead is the graveyard of the six races. There are no lawful cemeteries in the Middle Worlds. There have been times when the House of Life has called upon us for hosts and for parts. There have been other occasions when they have shipped us their excess."

"It is difficult to understand. It seems brutal, it seems harsh . . ."

"It is life and it is death. It is the greatest blessing and the greatest curse in the universe. You do not have to understand it, Wakim. Your comprehension or your lack of it, your approval or your disapproval, will in no way alter its operation."

"And whence come you, Anubis—and Osiris—that you control it?"

"There are some things that are not for you to know."

"And how do the Middle Worlds accept your control?"

"They live with it, and they die with it. It is above their objections, for it is necessary for their continued existence. It is become a natural law, and it is utterly impartial, applying with equal force to all who come beneath it."

"There are some who do not?"

"You shall learn more of this when I am ready to tell you, which is not now. I have made you a machine, Wakim. Now I shall make you a man. Who is to say how you started, where you started? Were I to wipe out your memories up to this moment and then re-embody you, you would recollect that you had begun as metal."

"Will you do this thing?"

"No. I want you equipped with the memories which you now possess, when and if I assign you to your new duties."

Then Anubis rasises his hands and strikes them together.

A machine removes Wakim from the shelf and switches off his senses as it lowers him. The music pulses and falls about the dancers, the two hundred torches blaze upon the pillars like immortal thoughts, Anubis stares at a blackened place upon the floor of the great Hall, and overhead the canopy of smoke moves to its own rhythms.

Wakim opens his eyes and looks upon grayness. He lies on his back, staring upward. The tiles are cold beneath him, and there is a flickering of light off to his right. Suddenly, he clenches his left hand, feels for his thumb, finds it, sighs.

"Yes," says Anubis.

He sits up before the throne, looks down upon himself, looks up at Anubis.

"You have been baptized, you have been born again into the flesh."

"Thank you."

"No trouble. Plenty of raw materials around here. Stand up! Do you remember your lessons?"

Wakim stands.

"Which ones?"

"Temporal fugue. To make time follow the mind, not the body."

"Yes."

"And killing?"

"Yes."

"And combining the two?"

17

"Yes."

Anubis stands, a full head taller than Wakim, whose new body is well over two yards in length.

"Then show me!"

"Let the music cease!" he cries. "Let the one who in life was called Dargoth come before me!"

The dead stop dancing. They stand without moving and their eyes never blink. There is silence for several seconds, unbroken by word, footfall, breathing.

Then Dargoth moves among the standing dead, advancing through shadow, through torchlight. Wakim stands straighter when he sees him, for the muscles of his back, his shoulders, his stomach tighten.

A metal band the color of copper crosses Dargoth's head, covers his cheekbones, vanishes beneath his gray-grizzled chin. A latitudinal band passes above his brows, over his temples, meets at the back of his skull. His eyes are wide, the sclera yellow and the irises red. His lower jaw makes a constant chewing motion as he rolls forward, and his teeth are long shadows. His head sways from side to side upon its twenty inches of neck. His shoulders are three feet in width, giving him the appearance of an inverted triangle, for his sides taper sharply to meet with his segmented chassis, which begins where the flesh stops. His wheels turn slowly, the left rear one squeaking with each revolution. His arms hang a full four and a half feet, so that his fingertips barely brush the floor. Four short, sharp metal legs are folded upward along his flat sides. The razors come erect on his back, fall again, as he moves. The eight-foot whip that is his tail uncoils behind him as he comes to a halt before the throne.

"For this night, this Thousandyear Night," says Anubis, "I give you back your name—Dargoth. Once were you numbered among the mightiest warriors in the Middle Worlds, Dargoth, until you pitted your strength against that of an immortal and went down to your death before him. Your broken body has been repaired, and this night you must use it to do battle once more. Destroy this man Wakim in single combat and you may take his place as my first servant here in the House of the Dead."

Dargoth crosses his great hands upon his brow and bows until they touch the floor.

"You may have ten seconds," says Anubis to Wakim, "to prepare your mind for battle. —Stand ready, Dargoth!"

"Lord," says Wakim, "how may I kill one who is already dead?"

"That is your problem," says Anubis. "You have now wasted all ten of your seconds with foolish questions. Begin!"

There comes a snapping sound and a series of metallic clicks.

Dargoth's metal legs snap downward, straighten, raise him three feet higher above the floor. He prances. He raises his arms and flexes them.

Wakim watches, waiting.

Dargoth rises onto his hind legs, so that now his head is ten feet above the floor.

Then he leaps forward, his arms outstretched, his tail curled, his head extended, fangs bared. The blades rise upon his back like gleaming fins, his hooves fall like hammers.

At the last possible moment, Wakim sidesteps and throws a punch which is blocked by the other's forearm. Wakim leaps high into the air then, and the whip cracks harmlessly beneath him.

For all his bulk, Dargoth halts and turns rapidly. He rears once more and strikes forward with his front hooves. Wakim avoids them, but Dargoth's hands fall upon Wakim's shoulders as Dargoth descends.

Wakim seizes both wrists and kicks Dargoth in the chest. The tail-lash falls across his right cheek as he does so. Then he breaks the grip of those massive hands upon his shoulder, ducks his head and lays the edge of his left hand hard upon the other's side. The whip falls again, this time across his back. He aims a blow at the other's head, but the long neck twists it out of the way, and he hears the whip crack once more, missing him by inches.

Dargoth's fist lands upon his cheekbone, and he stumbles, off balance, sliding upon the floor. He rolls out of the path of the hooves, but a fist knocks him sprawling as he attempts to rise again.

As the next blow descends, however, he catches the wrist with both hands and throws his full weight upon the arm, twisting his head to the side. Dargoth's fist strikes the floor and Wakim regains his feet, landing a left cross as he does so.

Dargoth's head rolls with the punch and the lash cracks beside Wakim's ear. He lays another blow upon the twisting head, and then he is borne over backwards as Dargoth's rear legs straighten like springs and his shoulder strikes Wakim in the chest.

Dargoth rears once more.

Then, for the first time, he speaks:

"Now, Wakim, now!" he says, "Dargoth becomes first servant of Anubis!"

As the hooves flash downward, Wakim catches those metal legs, one in each hand, halfway up their length. He has braced himself in a crouched position, and now his lips curl back, showing his clenched teeth, as Dargoth is frozen in mid-strike above him.

He laughs as he springs back into a standing position and heaves with both arms, casting his opponent high up upon his hind legs, struggling to keep from falling over backwards.

"Fool!" he says, and his voice is strangely altered. His word, like the stroke of a great iron bell, rings through the Hall. There comes up a soft moaning from among the dead, as when they had been routed from out their graves.

"'Now,' you say? 'Wakim,' you say?" and he laughs as he steps forward beneath the falling hooves. "You know not what you say!" and he locks his arms about the great metal torso and the hooves flail helplessly above his back and the tail-whip swishes and cracks and lays stripes upon his shoulders. His hands rest between the sharpened spines, and he crushes the unyielding segmented body of metal close up against his own.

Dargoth's great hands find his neck, but the thumbs cannot reach his throat, and the muscles of Wakim's neck tighten and stand out as he bends his knees and strains.

They stand so, frozen for a timeless instant, and the firelight wrestles with shadows upon their bodies.

Then with a gigantic, heaving motion, Wakim raises Dargoth above the ground, turns, and hurls him from him.

Dargoth's legs kick wildly as he turns over in the air. His spines rise and fall and his tail reaches out and cracks. He raises his arms up before his face, but he lands with a shattering crash at the foot of the throne of Anubis, and there he lies still, his metal body broken in four places and his head split open upon the first step to the throne.

Wakim turns toward Anubis.

"Sufficient?" he inquires.

"You did not employ temporal fugue," says Anubis, not even looking downward at the wreck that had been Dargoth.

"It was unnecessary. He was not that mighty an opponent."

"He was mighty," says Anubis. "Why did you laugh, and make as if you questioned your name when you fought with him?"

"I do not know. For a moment, when I realized that I could not be beaten, I felt as though I were someone else."

"Someone without fear, pity, or remorse?"

"Yes."

"Do you still feel thus?"

"No."

"Then why have you stopped calling me 'Master'?"

"The heat of battle raised emotions which overrode my sense of protocol."

"Then correct the oversight, immediately."

"Very well, Master."

"Apologize. Beg my pardon, most humbly."

Wakim prostrates himself on the floor.

"I beg your pardon, Master. Most humbly."

"Rise again, and consider yourself pardoned. The contents of your previous stomach have gone the way of all such things. You may go re-refresh yourself now. —Let there be singing and dancing once more! Let there be drinking and laughter in celebration of the name-giving on this, Wakim's Thousand-year Eve! Let the carcass of Dargoth be gone from my sight!"

And these things are done.

After Wakim finishes his meal, and it seems as if the dancing and the singing of the dead will continue until Time's well-deserved end, Anubis gestures, first to his left, then to his right, and every other flame folds upon every other pillar, dives within itself, is gone. His mouth opens and the words come down upon Wakim: "Take them back. Fetch me my staff."

Wakim stands and gives the necessary orders. Then he leads the dead out from the great Hall. As they depart, the tables vanish between the pillars. An impossible breeze tears at the ceiling of smoke. Before that great, gray mat is shredded, however, the other torches have died, and the only illumination within the Hall comes from the two blazing bowls on either side of the throne.

Anubis stares into the darkness, and the captured light-rays reform themselves at his bidding and he sees Dargoth fall once more at the foot of his throne and lie still, and he sees the one he has named Wakim standing with a skull's grin upon his lips, and for an instant—had it been a trick of the firelight?—a mark upon his brow.

Far, in an enormous room where the light is dim and orange and crowded into corners and the dead lay them down once more upon invisible cataflaques above their opened graves, faint, rising, then falling, Wakim hears a sound that is not like any sound he has ever heard before. He stays his hand upon the staff and descends the dais.

"Old man," he says to one with whom he spoke earlier, one whose hair and whose beard are stained with wine and in whose left wrist a clock has stopped, "old man, hear my words and tell me if you know: What is that sound?"

The unblinking eyes stare upward, past his own, and the lips move: "Master . . ."

"I am not Master here."

". . . Master, it is but the howling of a dog."

Wakim returns then to the dais and gives them all back to their graves.

Then the light departs and the staff guides him through the dark along the path that has been ordained.

"I have brought your staff, Master."

"Arise, and approach."

"The dead are all returned to their proper places."

"Very good. —Wakim, you are my man?"

"Yes, Master."

"To do my bidding, and to serve me in all things?"

"Yes, Master."

"This is why you are emissary to the Middle Worlds, and beyond."

"I am to depart the House of the Dead?"

"Yes, I am sending you forth from here on a mission."

"What sort of mission?"

"The story is long, involved. There are many persons in the Middle Worlds who are very old. You know this?"

"Yes."

"And there are some who are timeless and deathless."

"Deathless, Lord?"

"By one means or another, certain individuals have achieved a kind of immortality. Perhaps they follow the currents of life and draw upon their force, and they flee from the waves of death. Perhaps they have adjusted their biochemistry, or they keep their bodies in constant repair, or they have many bodies and exchange them, or steal new ones. Perhaps they wear metal bodies, or no bodies at all. Whatever the means involved, you will hear talk of the Three Hundred Immortals when you enter the Middle Worlds. This is only an approximate figure, for few truly know much about them. There are two hundred eighty-three immortals, to be exact. They cheat on life, on death, as you can see, and their very existence upsets the balance, inspires others to strive to emulate their legends, causes others to think them gods. Some are harmless wanderers, others are not. All are powerful and subtle, all adept at continuing their existence. One is especially noxious, and I am sending you to destroy him."

"Who may he be, Master?"

"He is called the Prince Who Was A Thousand, and he dwells beyond the Middle Worlds. His kingdom lies beyond the realm of life and death, in a place where it is always twilight. He is difficult to locate, however, for he often departs his own region and trespasses into the Middle Worlds and elsewhere. I desire that he come to an end, as he has opposed both the House of the Dead and the House of Life for many days."

"What does he look like, the Prince Who Was A Thousand?"

"Anything he wishes."

"Where shall I find him?"

"I do not know. You must seek him."

"How shall I know him?"

"By his deeds, by his words. He opposes us in all ways."

"Surely others must oppose you also . . ."

"Destroy all you come upon who do so. You shall know the Prince Who Was A Thousand, however, because he shall be the most difficult of all to destroy. He will come closest to destroying you."

"Suppose he succeeds."

"Then I shall take me a thousand years more to train another emissary to set upon this task. I do not desire his downfall today or tomorrow. It will doubtless take you centuries even to locate him. Time matters little. An age will pass before he becomes a threat, to Osiris or myself. You will learn of him as you travel, seeking after him. When you find him you *will* know him."

"Am I mighty enough to work his undoing?"

"I think you are."

"I am ready."

"Then I shall set your feet upon the track. I give you the power to summon me, and in times of need to draw force from the fields of Life and of Death while you are among the Middle Worlds. This will make you invincible. You will report back to me when you feel you need to. If I feel this need, I will reach out after you."

"Thank you, Master."

"You will obey all my sendings, instantly."

"Yes."

"Go now and rest. After you have slept and eaten again, you will depart and begin your mission."

"Thank you."

"This will be your second-last sleep within this House, Wakim. Meditate upon the mysteries it contains."

"I do so constantly."

"I am one of them."

"Master . . ."

"That is part of my name. Never forget it."

"Master—how could I?"

The Waking of the Red Witch

The Witch of the Loggia stirs in her sleep and cries out twice. Long has she slept now, and deeply. Her familiar rushes to comfort her, but bungles the job and causes her to awaken. She sits up then among cushions in her cathedral-high hall, and Time with Tarquin's ravishing stride from her divan moves like a ghost, but she sees him and freezes him in his trackless-ness with a gesture and a word, and hears then her doubled cry and looks backward with her eyes upon the dreamdark scream-sought thing she'd borne. Let there be ten cannon crashes and remove them from the air and the ear, preserving the nine crowded silences that lie between. Let these be heartbeats, then, and felt throughout the body mystical. In this still center, place a dry skin which has sloughed its snake. Now, let there be no moaning at the bar should a sunken ship return to port. Instead, withdraw from the dreamdark thing, with its rain like rapid-fire rosaries of guilt, cold and untold upon your belly. Think instead of broken horses, the curse of the Dutchman, and perhaps a line by the mad poet Vramin, such as, "The bulb resurrects the daffodil, within its season." If you ever loved anything in your life, try to remember it. If you ever betrayed anything, pretend for a moment that you have been forgiven. If you ever feared anything, pretend for an instant that those days are gone and will never return. Buy the lie and hold to it for as long as you can. Press your familiar, whatever its name, to your breast and stroke it till it purrs.

Trade life and death for oblivion, but light or dark will reach your bones or your flesh. Morning will come, and with it remembrance.

The Red Witch sleeps within her cathedral-high hall, between the past and the future. Her fleeing rapist of a dream disappears down dark alleyways, while Time ticks history around events. And she smiles now as she sleeps, for Janus is again doing things by halves. . . .

Backward-turned to glory, she dwells in his warm, green gaze.

Death, Life,
the Magician and Roses

Listen to the world. It is called Blis, and it is not hard to hear at all: The sounds may be laughter, sighs, contented belches. They may be the *clog-clog* of machinery or beating hearts. They may be the breathing of multitudes or their words. They may be footsteps, footsteps, the sound of a kiss, a slap, the cry of a baby. Music. Music, perhaps. The sound of typewriter keys through the Black Daddy Night, consciousness kissing paper only? Perhaps. Then forget the sounds and the words and look at the world.

First, colors: Name one. Red? There's a riverbank that color, green stream hauled between, snagged on purple rocks. Yellow and gray and black is the city in the distance. Here in the open field, both sides of the river, are pavilions. Pick any color—they're all about. Over a thousand pavilions, like balloons and tepees and stemless mushrooms, blazing in the midst of a blue field, strung with pennons, full of moving colors that are people. Three lime-bright bridges span the river. The river leads to a creamy sea which swells but seldom breaks. From it, up the river, come barges and boats and other vessels which moor along the banks. More come out of the sky, settling anywhere upon the blue fabric of the field. Their passengers move among the pavilions. They are of all races and sorts. They eat and they talk. They play. They are making the sounds and wearing the colors. Okay?

The odors are of sweet and growing things and kissful come the breezes. When these breezes and these odors reach the fairground, they are altered subtly. There comes up the odor of sawdust, which is hardly unpleasant; and that of perspiration, which cannot be too unpleasant if some of it is your own. Then there are smells of wood-smoke, smells of food, and the clean aroma of alcohol. Smell the world. Taste it, swallow it and hold it in your belly. Burst with it.

. . . Like the man with the eyepatch and the alpenstock.

He walks among the hucksters and the fillies, fat as a eunuch, but not. His flesh is strangely flesh-colored, and his right eye is a gray wheel, rolling. A week's growth of beard frames his face, and all colors are missing from the blot of his garments. His gait is steady. His hands are hard.

He stops to buy a mug of beer, moves to watch a cockfight.

He wagers a coin on the smaller bird, which tears the larger apart and so pays for his beer.

He watches the deflowering-show, samples the narcotics exhibit, foils a brown man in a white shirt who attempts to guess his weight. A short man with close-set dark eyes then emerges from a nearby tent, moves his side, tugs upon his sleeve.

"Yes?" His voice seems centrally located, that deeply potent does it stir.

"I see by your outfit you may be a preacher."

"Yes, I am—of the non-theistic, non-sectarian sort."

"Very good. Would you care to earn some money? It will only take a few moments."

"What would you have me do?"

"A man is going to commit suicide and be buried in that tent. The grave is already dug and all the tickets have been sold. The audience is growing restless now, though. The performer won't do it without proper religious accompaniment, and we can't sober up the preacher."

"I see. It will cost you ten."

"Make it five?"

"Get yourself another preacher."

"All right ten! C'mon! They're starting to clap their hands and boo!"

He moves into the tent, blinks his eyes.

"Here's the preacher!" calls out the emcee. "We're ready to go ahead now. —What'cher name, Dad?"

"Sometimes I'm called Madrak."

The man stops, turns and stares at him, licks his lips.

"I . . . didn't realize."

"Let's be on with it."

"Okay, sir. —Make way here! Coming through! Hot stuff!"

The crowd parts. There are perhaps three hundred people within the tent. Overhead lights blaze down upon a roped-in circle of bare earth in which a grave has been dug. Insects fly in rings through falling dust within the ladders of light. An opened coffin lies beside the opened grave. On a small platform of wood is a chair. The man seated upon the chair is perhaps fifty years of age. His face is flat and full of wrinkles, his complexion pale. His eyes bulge slightly. He wears only a pair of shorts, and he has much gray hair upon his chest, his arms, his legs. He leans forward and squints as the two approach through the crowd.

"All set, Dolmin," says the small man.

"My ten," says Madrak.

The small man slips him a folded bill, which Madrak inspects and places in his wallet.

The small man climbs up onto the platform and smiles out

over the crowd. Then he pushes his straw hat back upon his head.

"All right, folks," he begins, "now we're all set to go. I know you'll find this was worth waiting for. As I announced earlier, this man Dolmin is about to commit suicide before your very eyes. For personal reasons he is resigning from the big race, and he has consented to earn a little money for his family by doing it in full sight of all. His performance will be followed by a genuine burial, in this same ground upon which you are now standing. It has doubtless been a long time since any of you have seen a real death—and I doubt anyone here present has ever seen a burial. So we're about ready to turn this show over to the preacher and Mister Dolmin. Let's have a nice hand for them both!"

There is applause within the tent.

". . . And a final word of caution. Do not stand too close. We are bending an ordnance, despite the fact that this tent has been fully fireproofed. Okay! Take it away!"

He jumps down from the platform as Madrak mounts it. Madrak leans toward the seated man as a can marked FLAMMABLE is placed beside his chair. "Are you sure you want to go through with this?" he asks the man.

"Yes."

He looks into the man's eyes, but the pupils are not enlarged, nor are they shrunken.

"Why?"

"Personal reasons, Dad. I'd rather not go into them. Shrive me, please."

Madrak places his hand upon the man's head.

"Insofar as I may be heard by anything, which may or may not care what I say, I ask, if it matters, that you be forgiven for anything you may have done or failed to do which requires forgiveness. Conversely, if not forgiveness but something else may be required to insure any possible benefit for which you may be eligible after the destruction of your body, I ask that this, whatever it may be, be granted or withheld, as the case may be, in such a manner as to insure your receiving said benefit. I ask this in my capacity as your elected intermediary between yourself and that which may not be yourself, but which may have an interest in the matter of your receiving as much as it is possible for you to receive of this thing, and which may in some way be influenced by this ceremony. Amen."

"Thank you, Dad."

"Beautiful!" sobs a fat woman with blue wings, from the front row.

The man called Dolmin raises the can marked FLAMMABLE, unscrews the cap, pours its contents over himself. "Has anyone got a cigarette?" he asks, and the small man hands one up to him. Dolmin reaches into the pocket of his shorts and withdraws a lighter. Then he pauses and looks out over the crowd. Someone calls out, "Why are you doing it?" He smiles then and replies, "A general protest against life, perhaps, which is a foolish game, is it not? Follow me. . . ." Then he lights the lighter. By this time, Madrak is well outside the roped-in circle.

A blast of heat follows the blaze, and the single scream is a hot nail driven through everything.

The six men who are standing by with fire extinguishers relax when they see that the flames will not spread.

Madrak folds his hands beneath his chin and rests them upon his staff.

After a time, the flames go out and the men with asbestos gloves come forward to handle the remains. The audience is quiet. There has been no applause thus far.

"So that's what it's like!" someone finally whispers, and the words carry throughout the tent.

"Perhaps," comes a precise, cheerful voice from the back of the tent, "and perhaps not, also."

Heads turn as the speaker moves forward. He is tall and has a pointed green beard and matching eyes and hair. His complexion is pale, his nose long and thin. He wears black and green.

"It is the magician," someone says, "from the show across the river."

"Correct," he replies, with a nod and a smile, and he makes his way forward through the crowd, clearing his path with a silver-topped cane. The lid is closed on the casket as he pauses and whispers, "Madrak the Mighty."

Madrak turns and says, "I've been looking for you."

"I know. That's why I'm here. What is this silly business?"

"Suicide show," says Madrak. "A man named Dolmin. They've forgotten what death is like."

"So soon, so soon," sighs the other. "Then let us give them their money's worth—full circle!"

"Vramin, I know you can do it, but considering the shape he's in—"

The small man in the straw hat approaches and regards them with his small, dark eyes.

"Sir," he says to Madrak, "any other ceremonial things you'd care to do before the interment?"

"I—"

"Of course not," says Vramin. "One only buries the dead."

"What do you mean?"

"That man is not dead—only smoldering."

"You're wrong, mister. This is an honest show."

"Nevertheless, I say he lives and will walk again for your amusement."

"You must be some kind of 'chotic."

"Only an humble thaumaturge," Vramin replies, stepping into the circle.

Madrak follows him. Vramin then raises his cane and weaves it through a cryptic gesture. It glows with green light, which then leaps forward and falls upon the box.

"Dolmin, come forth!" says Vramin.

The audience presses forward. Vramin and Madrak move to the wall of the tent. The small man would follow them, but is distracted by a knocking from within the coffin.

"Brother, we'd best leave," says Vramin, and slices through the fabric with the tip of his cane.

The lid of the coffin is slowly raised as they step through the wall and into the world without.

Beyond them a sound occurs. It is compounded of screaming and cries of "Fake!" and "We want our money back!" and "*Look* at him!"

" 'What fools these mortals be,' " says the green man, who is one of the few persons living able to put quotation marks around it and know why.

He is coming, riding down the sky on the back of a great beast of burnished metal. It has eight legs and its hooves are diamonds. Its body is as long as two horses. Its neck is as long as its body, and its head is that of a Chinese demon dog out of gold. Beams of blue light come forth from its nostrils and its tail is three antennae. It moves across the blackness that lies between the stars, and its mechanical legs move slowly. Each step that it takes, however, crossing from nothing to nothing, carries it twice the distance of the previous step. Each stride also takes the same amount of time as the prior one. Suns flash by, fall behind, wink out. It runs through solid matter, passes through infernos, pierces nebulae, faster and faster moving through the starfall blizzard in the forest of the night. Given a sufficient warm-up run, it is said that it could circumnavigate the universe in a single stride. What would happen if it kept running after that, no one knows.

Its rider was once a man. He is the one who is called the Steel General. That is not a suit of armor that he is wearing; it is his body. He has turned off most of his humanity for the duration of the trip, and he stares now straight ahead past the scales like bronze oak leaves on the side of his mount's neck. He holds four reins, each as thick as a strand of silk, on the fingertips of his left hand. He wears a ring of tanned human flesh on his little finger, because it would be senselss and noisy for him to wear metal jewelry. The flesh was once his; at least, it helped to surround him at one time long ago.

Wherever his goes, he carries a collapsible five-string banjo with him in a compartment near to where his heart used to be. When he plays it he becomes a kind of negative Orpheus and men follow him to Hell.

He is also one of the very few masters of temporal fugue in the entire universe. It is said that no man can lay hands upon him unless he permits it.

His mount was once a horse.

Regard the world of Blis, with its color and its laughter and its breezes. Regard the world of Blis as Megra of Kalgan.

Megra is a nurse in Kalgan Obstetrical Center 73, and she knows that the world is babies. Blis has something like ten billion people breathing at one another, with more occurring constantly and very few departing. The impaired are repaired. There is no infant mortality. Screams of the newborn and the laughter of their makers are the two most often heard sounds on Blis.

Megra of Kalgan regards Bliss through cobalt-colored eyes amidst long blonde lashes. The fine strands of her pale hair tickle her naked shoulders, and two stiffened spears of it cross to form an X in the center of her brow. Her nose is small, her mouth is a tiny blue flower, and she has very little chin to speak of. She wears a silver breast strap, a golden belt and a short silver skirt. She is barely five feet in height, and she has been touched with the odor of flowers she has never seen. She wears a golden pendant which grows warm upon her breast whenever men place aphrodisiacs before her.

Megra waited ninety-three days before she could gain entrance to the Fair. The waiting list was long, because of the fact that the fairground that is all colors and odors and movements is one of the very few such open places remaining upon Blis. There are only fourteen cities on Blis, but they cover the four continents from sea to creamy sea, burrow far beneath the land and tower into the sky. Portions of them also extend beneath the seas. Actually, all of them interlock with several others, making for continental layers of civilization; but since there are fourteen separate city governments with clear territorial jurisdictions, there are said to be fourteen cities on Blis. Megra's city is Kalgan, where she tends life that is screaming and new, and occasionally life that is screaming and old, in all colors, all shapes. Since a gene pattern can be constructed to satisfy the parents' specific wishes and substituted surgically for the nucleus of a fertilized cell, she is liable to see anything born and often does. Being old-fashioned, all that Megra's own parents had wanted was a cobalt-eyed doll with the strength of a dozen or so men, so that the kid could take care of herself in life.

However, after having taken care of herself successfully for eighteen years, Megra decided that the time had come to contribute to the general breathing. It takes two to strive for infinity, and Megra decided upon the colors and the romance of the open places, of the fairground, for her striving. Life is her occupation and her religion, and she is anxious to serve it further. A month's vacation lies before her.

All she has to do now is find the other one. . . .

The Thing That Cries In The Night raises its voice within its barless prison. It howls, coughs and barks, gibbers, wails. It is contained within a silver cocoon of fluctuating energies, suspended from an invisible web of forces and hung within a place which has never known daylight.

The Prince Who Was A Thousand tickles it with laser beams,

bathes it with gamma rays and feeds it a varying range of ultrasonics and subsonics.

Then it is silent, and for a bare moment the Prince raises his head from the equipment he has brought, and his green eyes widen and the corners of his thin lips twitch upwards after a smile they never reach.

It begins to scream again.

He gnashes his milk-white teeth and throws back his dark cowl.

His hair is a halo of fallow gold in the twilight of the Place Without Doors. He stares upward at the almost-seen form that writhes within the light. As often he has cursed it, his lips move mechanically around the words they always form when he fails.

For ten centuries he has tried to kill it, and still it lives.

He crosses his arms upon his breast, bows his head and vanishes.

A dark thing cries out within the light, within the night.

Madrak tilts the beaker, refills their glasses.

Vramin raises his, stares out across the wide esplanade before his pavilion, quaffs it.

Madrak pours once more.

"It is neither life, nor is it fair," says Vramin, finally.

"Yet you never actively supported the program."

"What matters that? It is my present feelings that control me."

"The feelings of a poet . . ."

Vramin strokes his beard.

"I can never give full allegiance to anything or to anyone," he replies.

"Pity, poor Angel of the Seventh Station."

"That title perished with the Station."

"In exile, the aristocracy always tends to preserve small items pertaining to rank."

"Face yourself in the darkness and what do you see?"

"Nothing."

"Exactly."

"What is the connection?"

"Darkness."

"I fail to see."

"That, warrior-priest, is common in the dark."

"Cease the riddling, Vramin. What is the matter?"

"Why did you seek me, here at the Fair?"

"I have the latest population figures with me. They strike me as approximating the mythical Point Critical—that which never occurs. Would you care to see them?"

"No. I do not need to. Whatever the figures, your conclusion is correct."

"You feel it with your special perceptions, within the tides of the Power?"

Vramin nods.

"Give me a cigarette," says Madrak.

Vramin gestures, and a lighted cigarette appears between his fingers.

"It is special this time," he says. "It is not just a waning of the tide of Life. There will be a rip tide, I fear."

"How will this be manifest?"

"I do not know, Madrak. But I do not intend to stay here longer than is necessary to find out."

"Oh? When will you depart?"

"Tomorrow evening, though I know I am flirting with the Black Tide once more. I had best do something about my death wish again, sometime soon, preferably in pentameter."

"Do any others remain?"

"No, we are the only two immortals on Blis."

"Will you give me a gateway when you go?"

"Of course."

"Then I'll remain here at the Fair until tomorrow evening."

"I should strongly recommend your going immediately, rather than waiting. I can provide a gateway now." Vramin gestures again and draws upon a cigarette of his own. He notices his refilled glass and sips it. "It would be an act of wisdom to depart immediately," he decides, "but wisdom is itself the product of knowledge; and knowledge, unfortunately, is generally the product of foolish doings. So, to add to my own knowledge and to enhance my wisdom I shall remain another day, to see what occurs."

"Then you expect that something special will happen tomorrow?"

"Yes. The rip tide. I feel the coming of Powers. There was recently some movement in that great House where all things go."

"Then this is knowledge which I, too, wish to obtain," says Madrak, "as it affects my former master Who Was A Thousand."

"You cling to an outworn loyalty, mighty one."

"Perhaps. And what is your excuse? Why do you seek to enhance your wisdom at this expense?"

"Wisdom is an end in itself. Also, these doings may be sources of great poetry."

"If death be the source of great poetry, then I prefer the lesser variety. I feel, though, that the Prince should know of any new development within the Middle Worlds."

"I drink to your loyalty, old friend, though I feel our former liege to be at least partly responsible for the present muddle."

"Your feelings on this matter are not unknown to me."

The poet takes one sip and lowers his glass. His eyes then grow all of one color, that being green. The white which encircles them vanishes, and the black points are gone that had been their centers. They are now become pale emeralds, and a yellow spark lives within each.

"Speaking in my capacity as mage and seer," he says, in a voice grown distant and toneless, "I say that it has now arrived upon Blis, this thing that portends the chaos. I say, too, that another comes, for I hear soundless hoofbeats within the dark, and I see that which is invisible in its many-strided pacings over stars. We may yet ourselves be drawn into this thing, who have no wish to participate."

"Where? And how?"

"Here. And it is not life, nor is it fair."

Madrak nods his head and says, "Amen."

The magician gnashes his teeth. "It is our destiny to bear witness," he decides, and his eyes burn with an infernal brilliance and his knuckles whiten upon the black walking stick with its head of silver.

. . . An eunuch priest of the highest caste sets tapers before a pair of old shoes.

. . . The dog worries the dirty glove which has seen many better centuries.

. . . The blind Norns strike a tiny silver anvil with fingers that are mallets. Upon the metal lies a length of blue light. The mirror comes alive with images of nothing that stands before it.

It hangs in a room which has never held furniture, hangs upon a wall covered with dark tapestries, hangs before the witch who is red, and her flames.

Looking into it is like looking through a window into a room filled with pink cobwebs which are stirred by sudden gusts of air.

Her familiar stands upon her right shoulder, its hairless tail hung about her neck, between her breasts. She strokes its head and it wags its tail.

She smiles, and the cobwebs slowly blow away. The flames leap about her, but nothing is burning.

Then the cobwebs are gone and she regards the colors of Blis.

41

Most particularly, though, she regards the tall man who stands naked to the waist in the midst of a thirty-five-foot circle surrounded by people.

His shoulders are wide, and his waist is quite narrow. He is barefooted, and he wears tight black trousers. He stares downward. His hair is sand-colored; his arms are enormously well muscled; his skin is rather pale. About his waist goes a wide, dark belt with a vicious row of studs set upon it. He stares downward through yellow eyes at the man who is attempting to raise himself from where he lies upon the ground.

The man at his feet is heavy about the shoulders, chest, stomach. He raises himself with one arm. His beard brushes his shoulder as he throws back his head and glares upward. His lips move, but his teeth are clenched.

The standing man moves one foot, almost casually, sweeping away the supporting arm. The other falls upon his face and does not move.

After a time, two men enter the circle and bear away the man who has fallen.

"Who?" pipes the familiar.

The Red Witch shakes her head, however, and continues to watch.

A four-armed man enters the circle, and his feet are great, splayed things, like another pair of enormous hands at the bottoms of his twisted legs. He is hairless and shining, and as he draws near to the standing man, he drops so that his lower arms come to rest upon the ground. As he does so, his knees turn outward to the sides and he bends backward, so that his head and his shoulders are still perpendicular to the ground, though now at a height of approximately three feet above it.

Springing froglike, he does not encounter his target, but meets instead with a flat hand upon the back of his neck and another beneath his stomach. Each hand describes a semicircle, and he passes, head over hands over hands over heels.

But he crouches where he falls, his sides heave three times and he leaps once more.

This time the tall man catches his ankles and holds him upside down at arm's length from his body.

But the four-armed man twists and seizes the wrists which hold him, driving his head into the other's stomach. There is blood upon his scalp then, for he has struck one of the belt studs, but the tall man does not release him. He pivots upon his heel and swings him outward. Then he turns again and again, until he moves like a top, spinning. After a full minute he slows, and the four-armed man's eyes are closed. Then he lowers him to the ground, falls upon him, moves his hands quickly, rises. The four-armed man lies still. After a time, he, too, is taken away.

Three more than fall before him, including Blackthorn Villy, Fourcity Champion of Blis, with his mechanical pincers, and the man is taken up upon shoulders and garlanded, and they bear him to a platform and honor him with the cup of victory and the draft of money. He does not smile until his eyes fall upon Megra of Kalgan, standing there, whose blonde X marks the spot his glances go to till he is free to follow them with boots upon his feet.

She waits for this.

The Red Witch watches the lips of the multitudes.

"Wakim," she finally says. "They call him Wakim."

"Why is it that we watch him?"

"I had a dream which I have read to indicate this: *Watch the place of the changing tide.* Even here, beyond the Middle Worlds, the mind of a witch is tied to the tides of the Power. Though I cannot use them now, still do I perceive them."

"Why this one—this Wakim—at the place of the changing tide?"

"The quality of the mirror is mute omniscience. It shows anything, explains nothing. But it took its direction from my

43

dream, so it remains for me to interpret this thing through meditation."

"He is strong, and very fast."

"True, I have not seen his like since sun-eyed Set fell before the Hammer That Smashes Suns, in his battle with the Nameless. Wakim is more than he appears to that crowd, or to the little girl toward whom he moves. See, as I cause the mirror to brighten and brighten! There is a dark aura about him that I do not like. He is something of the reason my sleep was troubled. We must see that he is followed. We must learn what he is."

"He will take the girl over the hill," says her familiar, poking its cold nose into her ear. "Oh, let us watch!"

"Very well," she says, and it wags its tail and clasps its forepaws atop its curly head.

The man stands in a place that is circled round about with a pink hedge and filled with flowers of all colors. It contains benches, couches, chairs, a table and high trellises of roses, all beneath a great green umbrella tree that shuts out the sky. It is filled with perfumes and the essences of flowers, and there is music that hangs awhile upon the air and passes slowly through it. Pale lights move within the branches of the tree. A tiny, intoxicating fountain sparkles beside the table at the foot of the tree.

The girl closes the gate within the hedge. A sign saying "Do Not Disturb" begins to glow on its outer side. She moves toward the man.

"Wakim . . ." she says.

"Megra," he replies.

"Do you know why I asked you to come here?"

"This *is* a love garden," he says, "and I think I understand the customs of the country . . ."

She smiles, removes her breast strap then, hangs it upon a bush and places her hands on his shoulders.

He moves to draw her to him, does not succeed.

"You are strong, little girl."

"I brought you here to wrestle," she says.

He glances toward a blue couch, then back to the girl, a small smile occurring upon his lips.

She shakes her head, slowly.

"Not as you think. First must you defeat me in battle. I want no ordinary man, whose back might be broken by my embrace. Nor do I want a man who will tire after an hour, or three. I want a man whose strength flows like a river, endless. Are you that man, Wakim?"

"You saw me in battle."

"What of that? My strength is greater than that of any man I have ever known. Even now you are increasing your efforts to draw me to you, and you are not succeeding."

"I do not wish to hurt you, child."

And she laughs and breaks his grip upon her wrist, drawing his arm over her shoulder and seizing his thigh in a version of the *nage-waza* that is called *kata-garuma*, and hurling him across the love garden.

He comes to his feet and faces her. Then he removes his shirt that was white, drawing it up over his head. He reaches high and places it upon a limb of the great tree.

She comes forward and stands before him.

"Now you will fight with me?"

In answer, he snaps a rose from the trellis and offers it to her.

She draws her elbows far back, tightening her fists at her sides. Then both her arms drive forward, fists twisting in twin blows which strike him in the abdomen.

"I take it that you do not want the flower," he gasps, dropping it.

Her eyes flash blue fire as she steps upon the rose.

"Now will you fight with me?"

"Yes," he says. "I will teach you a hold that is called 'The

Kiss,'" and he takes her in a mighty embrace and crushes her to him. His mouth finds hers, though she twists her head to the side, and he straightens, raising her above the ground. She cannot breathe within his embrace, nor break it; and their kiss lasts until her strength slackens, and he carries her to the couch and lays her upon it.

There are roses, roses, roses, music, moving lights, a flower that has been broken.

Now the Red Witch is weeping softly.

Her familiar does not understand.

It will, though, soon.

The mirror is filled with man upon woman and woman by man.

They regard the movements of Blis.

Interlude in
the House of Life

Osiris sits in the House of Life, drinking the blood-red wine. The green glow fills the air about, and nowhere is there anything sharp or cold. He sits in the Hall of the Hundred Tapestries, and the walls are invisible behind them all. The floor is covered with a fabric that is thick and soft and golden in color.

He puts down an empty glass and stands. Moving across the Hall, he comes to the green tapestry, raises it, and steps into the cubicle which it conceals. He touches three of the coordination plates set in the wall, pushes aside the tapestry, and steps into a room located 348 miles south-southwest of the Hall of the Hundred Tapestries, at a depth of 78,544 feet.

The chamber he enters is semidark, but a portion of the green glow can be felt within it.

The one who wears a red loincloth and sits cross-legged upon the floor does not appear to notice him. His back is turned and he does not move. His body is normally formed, somewhat slim, and his muscles seem those of a swimmer. His hair is thick and as dark as hair can be without being black.

His complexion is pale. He is leaning forward and does not appear to be breathing.

Suddenly, another is seated across from him, in an identical posture. He is dressed in exactly the same manner. His complexion, hair, and musculature are the same. He *is* the same, in all respects; and he raises his dark eyes from the small yellow crystal they contemplate. Looking up, he sees the orange, green, yellow and black bird-head of Osiris, and his eyes widen and he says, "I have done it again," and the one whose back is to Osiris vanishes before him.

He scoops up the crystal, places it in a cloth bag with drawstrings and hangs it at his waist. Then he stands.

"Nine-second fugue," he says.

"Is that your record?" asks Osiris, and his voice sounds like a scratched recording that is being played too rapidly.

"Yes, father."

"Can you control it yet?"

"No."

"How much longer will it take?"

"Who knows? Ishibaka says perhaps three centuries."

"Then you will be a master?"

"No one can really tell in advance. There are fewer than thirty masters in all the worlds. It has taken me two centuries to advance this far, and it has been less than a year since the first movement. Of course, once it is developed, the power continues to grow. . . ."

Osiris shakes his head and steps forward, laying his hand upon his shoulder.

"Horus, my son and avenger, there is a thing I would have you do. It would be good if you were a master of the fugue, but it is not essential. Your other powers should prove sufficient to the task."

"What task is this, my father?"

"Your mother, wishing to gain once more my favor and a

48

return from exile, has offered me further information as to my colleague's activities. It appears that Anubis has sent a new emissary into the Middle Worlds, doubtless to locate our ancient enemy and destroy him."

"This would seem a good thing," says Horus, nodding, "if successful. I have my doubts, though, since he has failed each time he has tried. How many has he sent now—five or six?"

"Six. This one he has named Wakim is seventh."

"Wakim?"

"Yes, and the bitch tells me he seems to be something special."

"How so?"

"It is possible that the jackal spent a thousand years training him for this job. His fighting prowess may be equal to that of Madrak himself. And he appears to bear a special token none of the others bore. It would seem that he is attuned to draw energy directly from the field."

"I wonder how he thought that one up?" asks Horus, smiling.

"It would seem that he has been studying the tricks certain of the immortals have used against us."

"What would you have me do? Assist him against your enemy?"

"No. I have decided that whichever of us succeeds in destroying the Prince Who Was A Thousand, that one will gain the support of his fallen Angels who are numbered among the immortals. The rest should follow. Those who do not, will doubtless enter the House of the Dead at the hands of their fellows. The time is right. The old loyalties have been forgotten. A new, solitary liege would be welcomed, I feel, one who offered an end to their fugitive existence. And with the support of the immortals, one House can emerge supreme."

"I see your reasoning, father. It may well be that it is correct. You would have me find the Prince Who Was A Thousand before Wakim finds him, and slay him in the name of Life?"

49

"Yes, my avenger. Do you think you can do this?"

"I am troubled that you would ask that question, knowing my strengths."

"The Prince will be no easy prey. His strengths are mainly unknown, and I cannot tell you what he looks like, nor where he abides."

"I will find him. I will end him. But perhaps I had best destroy this Wakim before I begin the search."

"No! He is on the world of Blis, where even now the plague should be beginning. But do not approach that one, Horus! Not unless I bid it. I have strange feelings concerning Wakim. I must find out who he was before I permit such an attempt."

"Why is this, mighty father? What should that matter?"

"A memory of days before your days, which shall remain unspoken, returns to trouble me. Ask me no more."

"Very well."

"The bitch your mother bade me lay different plans concerning the Prince. If you should meet with her during your travels, do not be swayed by any counsels regarding leniency. The Prince must die."

"She would have him live?"

Osiris nods.

"Yes, she is very fond of him. She may have informed us of Wakim only to save the Prince from him. She will tell you any lie to gain her ends. Do not be deceived by such."

"I will not."

"Then I send you, Horus, my avenger and my son, as first emissary of Osiris into the Middle Worlds."

Horus bows his head and Osiris places his hand upon it for a warm moment.

"He is dead already," says Horus, slowly, "for was it not I that destroyed the Steel General himself?"

Osiris does not answer, for he, too, once destroyed the Steel General.

Dark Horse Shadow

In the great Hall of the House of the Dead there is an enormous shadow upon the wall, behind the throne of Anubis. It might almost be a decoration, inlaid or painted on, save that its blackness is absolute and seems to hold within it something of a limitless depth. Also, there is a slight movement to it.

It is the shadow of a monstrous horse, and the blazing bowls on either side of the throne do not affect it with their flickering light.

There is nothing in the great Hall to cast such a shadow, but had you ears in that place you could hear a faint breathing. With each audible exhalation the flames bow down, then rise again.

It moves slowly about the Hall and returns to rest upon the throne, blotting it completely from your sight, had you eyes in that place.

It moves without sound and it changes in size and shape as it goes on. It has a mane and a tail and four hooved legs in outline.

Then the sound of breathing comes again, like that of a mighty organ-bellows.

It rears to stand upon its hind legs, like a man, and its forelegs form the shadow of a slanted cross upon the throne.

There comes the sound of footsteps in the distance.

As Anubis enters, the Hall is filled by a mighty wind that ends with a snorted chuckle.

Then all is silent as the dog-headed one faces the shadow before his throne.

The Changing of the Tide

Regard the sounds of Blis: There are screams within the Life Fair.

A bloated body has been discovered in a guest pavilion.

Once it had been a man. Now it is a mottled sac which has burst itself in a dozen places and oozes juices upon the ground. Already it has begun to smell. This is the reason for its discovery.

It causes the screaming of a maid.

The screaming causes the crowd.

See how they mill about, asking one another the question they cannot answer?

They have forgotten what one does before the face of death.

Most of them will learn, shortly.

Megra of Kalgan pushes her way through the throng.

"I am a nurse," she says.

Most of them wonder at her action, for nurses have to do with babies, not stinking corpses.

53

The tall man at her side says nothing, but walks through the crowd as if it were not there.

Already, a small man in a straw hat has roped off the area and is beginning to sell tickets to those who would file past the remains. Megra asks the tall man, who is named Wakim, to stop him. Wakim smashes the admission machine and drives the man from the pavilion.

"He is dead," says Megra, regarding the body.

"Of course," says Wakim, who, after a thousand years in the House of the Dead, is readily able to recognize the condition. "Let us cover it over with the bedclothes."

"I know of no disease which behaves in such a manner."

"Then it must be a new disease."

"Something should be done. If it is contagious, an epidemic may follow."

"It will," says Wakim. "People will die rapidly, because it will spread at a rapid rate. There are so many people so crowded together in Blis that nothing can prevent this. Even if a cure is found in a matter of days, the population will doubtless be decimated."

"We must keep the corpse isolated, have it shipped to the nearest Obstetrical Center."

"If you wish. . . ."

"How can you be so indifferent in the face of tragedy?"

"Death is not tragic. Pathetic, perhaps, but not tragic. Let us cover it over with the bedclothes."

She slaps him with a sound that carries throughout the pavilion, and she turns away from him. Her eyes seek the communication ring on the wall; but as she steps toward it, a one-eyed man all in black stops her and says, "I have already called the nearest Center. An aircar is on the way."

"Thank you, Dad. Can you get these people out of here? They might be more inclined to listen to you."

He nods. Wakim covers the body. Megra turns to him once

more, as the one-eyed man bids the crowd depart and it moves to obey his words and his staff.

"How can you treat death so lightly?" she asks.

"Because it happens," he replies. "It is inevitable. I do not mourn the falling of a leaf or the breaking of a wave. I do not sorrow for a shooting star as it burns itself up in the atmosphere. Why should I?"

"Those things are not alive."

"Neither are men when they enter into the House of the Dead, and all things go there."

"That was long ago. None from Blis have gone to that place for many ages. It is a tragic thing when a life comes to an end."

"Life and death are not all that much different."

"You are a deviant from the social norm!" she announces, striking him again.

"Is that an insult or a diagnosis?" he asks.

There come then more screams from another part of the fairground.

"We must attend at once," she says, moving to depart.

"No!" He seizes her wrist.

"Let go of me!"

"I'm afraid I won't do that. You would serve no purpose by standing beside all the corpses which will occur here. You will further expose yourself, however, by doing this. I do not wish to lose a laymate such as yourself this quickly. I will take you back to the garden, where we will wait out the running of this thing. There is food there, and drink. We will put on the Do Not Disturb sign. . . ."

". . . And dally while the world dies? You are heartless!"

"Do you not wish to insure more lives, to replace some of those lost?"

She strikes him with her free hand, causing him to fall to one knee and raise his arm before him.

"Release me!" she cries.

"Let the lady go as she would." There are two other persons present in the pavilion. The one who has spoken is the warrior-priest Madrak, who remained after the crowd departed. At his side stands now the green magician known to men as Vramin.

Wakim stands and faces the two.

"Who are you?" he asks. "Who are you to give me orders?"

"I am known as Madrak, and called by some the Mighty."

"This means nothing to me. The order is not yours to give. Go away."

He catches Megra's other wrist, struggles with her briefly, raises her in his arms.

"I warn you. Release the lady." Madrak holds his staff before him as he speaks.

"Get out of my way, Madrak."

"I had best warn you before you continue that I am an immortal and that my strength has been heralded throughout the Middle Worlds. It was I who destroyed the centaur Dargoth, sending him down to ruin and the House of the Dead. Songs are still sung of that battle, which lasted a day and a night and a day."

Wakim lowers Megra to her feet and releases her.

"This does indeed make things different, immortal. I will attend to the girl in a moment. Tell me now, do you oppose the powers of the House of Life and the House of the Dead?"

Madrak gnaws for a moment upon the edge of his beard.

"Yes," he replies then. "What is that to you?"

"I am about to destroy you, and your friend beside you, if he is to be numbered among the two hundred eighty-three immortals."

The magician smiles and bows.

Megra departs the pavilion.

"The lady has escaped you," Vramin observes.

"It would seem, but I shall make it as if it had never occurred."

Then Wakim raises his left hand and advances upon Madrak.

Madrak's staff spins in his grip until it is nearly invisible, then strikes forward.

Wakim dodges the first blow, but the second one is laid upon his shoulder. He attempts to catch the staff, fails. A second blow falls upon him. He attempts to rush Madrak, but is caught by an horizontal moulinet across the chest. Then he falls back, crouches out of range, begins a shuffling circle about his opponent.

"How is it that you still stand?" asks Vramin, who stands aside, smoking.

"I cannot fall," Wakim replies.

He lunges then, but is beaten back once more.

Madrak moves to attack several times then, but on each occasion Wakim avoids the blow and attempts to seize the staff.

Finally, Wakim stops and retreats several paces.

"Enough of this foolishness! Time goes against my recovering the girl. You are good with that stick, fat Madrak, but it shall not help you now!"

Then, bowing his head slightly, Wakim vanishes from where he stands and Madrak lies upon the ground, his staff broken before him.

Wakim stands now at his side, his hand upraised as if recovering from a blow delivered.

The poet drops his cigarette and his cane leaps within his hands, tracing a circle of green fires about him. Wakim turns to face him.

"Fugue!" says Vramin. "A genuine fugue master! And forward-going! Who are you?"

"I am called Wakim."

"How is it that you know the exact number of the immortals, that being two hundred eighty-three?"

57

"I know what I know, and those flames will not save you."

"Perhaps, and perhaps not, Wakim. But I do not oppose the powers of the House of Life and the House of the Dead."

"You are an immortal. Your very existence is sufficient to give the lie to your words."

"I am too indifferent to oppose anything on principle. My life, however, is another matter," and his eyes flash green.

"Before you attempt to turn your power against me, Wakim, know that it is already too late. . . ."

He raises his cane.

"Either the dog or the bird has sent you, and it does not matter which. . . ."

Green fires spray in fountains upward, engulfing the pavilion.

"More than a mere plague-bearer, I know you to be. You are too well-endowed to be any less than an emissary. . . ."

The pavilion vanishes about them, and they stand in an open area in the midst of the Fair.

"Know that before you there have been others, and all of them have failed. . . ."

A green light leaps upward from his cane and arcs like a rocket flare through the sky.

"Two of them fell before the one who now approaches. . . ."

The light overhead persists, pulsates.

"Behold the one who comes upon scenes of chaos, and whose cold metal hand supports the weak and the oppressed."

He comes, riding down the sky on the back of a great beast of burnished metal. It has eight legs and its hooves are diamonds. It slows with each stride that it takes, covering less and less distance.

"He is called the Steel General, and he, too, is a fugue-master, Wakim. He hearkens to my beacon."

Wakim turns his eyes upward and beholds the one who had once been a man. Whether it is by Vramin's magic or some premonition of his own, he knows that this will be his first real contest in the thousand years of his memory.

The green fires fall upon Madrak now, and he stirs himself and rises with a moan.

Eight diamonds touch upon the ground, and Wakim hears the sound of a distant banjo.

The Red Witch calls for her Chariot of Ten, and orders her cloak of gold. This day she'll off across the sky to the Ring where the Midworlds go.

This day she'll off across the sky on her own wild ways to show. . . .

There, in the worlds of the Life and the Death, the worlds that she used to know.

Now, some say her name is Mercy and others say it's Lust. Her secret name is Isis. Her secret soul is dust.

. . . An eunuch priest of the highest caste sets tapers before a pair of old shoes.

. . . The dog worries the dirty glove which hath seen many better centuries.

. . . The blind Norns strike a tiny silver anvil with fingers that are mallets. Upon the metal lies a length of blue light.

Place of the Heart's Desire

The Prince Who Was A Thousand walks beside the sea and under the sea. The only other intelligent inhabitant of the world within which he walks cannot be sure whether the Prince created it or discovered it. This is because one can never be sure whether wisdom produces or merely locates, and the Prince is wise.

He walks along the beach. His footsteps begin seven paces behind him. High above his head hangs the sea.

The sea hangs above his head because it has no choice in the matter. The world within which he walks is so constructed that if one were to approach it from any direction, it would appear to be a world completely lacking in land masses. If one were to descend far enough beneath that sea which surrounds it, however, one would emerge from the underside of the waters and enter into the planet's atmosphere. Descending still farther, one would reach dry land. Traversing this land, one might come upon other bodies of water, waters bounded by land, beneath the sea that hangs in the sky.

The big sea flows perhaps a thousand feet overhead. Bright fish fill its bottom, like mobile constellations. And down here on the land, everything glows.

It has been said that a world such as this unnamed place with a sea for a sky could not possibly exist. Those who said it are obviously wrong. Positing infinity, the rest is easy.

The Prince Who Was A Thousand is in an unique position. He is a teleportationist, among other things, and this is even rarer than a master of temporal fugue. In fact, he is the only one of his kind. He can transport himself, in no time at all, to any place that he can visualize.

And he has a very vivid imagination. Granting that any place you can think of exists somewhere in infinity, if the Prince can think of it too, he is able to visit it. Now, a few theorists claim that the Prince's visualizing a place and willing himself into it is actually an act of creation. No one knew about the place before, and if the Prince can find it, then perhaps what he really did was make it happen. However—positing infinity, the rest is easy.

The Prince has not the least idea, not a snowball in hell's worth, as to where the nameless world is located, anyway, in relation to the rest of the universe. Nor does he care. He can come and go as he chooses, taking with him whomsoever he would.

He has come alone, however, because he wishes to visit his wife.

He stands beside the sea, beneath the sea, and he calls out her name, which is the name "Nephytha," and he waits till a breeze comes to him from across the waters, touching him and saying the name that is his own.

He bows then his head and feels her presence about him.

"How goes the world with thee, loved one?" he inquires.

There comes a sob upon the air, breaking the surf's monotone turning.

"Well," comes the reply. "And thyself, my lord?"

"I will be truthful rather than polite, and say 'poorly.'"

"It cries yet in the night?"

"Yes."

"I thought of thee as I drifted and as I flowed. I have made birds to be within the air to keep me company, but their cries are either harsh or sad. What may I tell thee, to be polite rather than truthful? That I am not sickened by this life that is not life? That I do not long to be a woman once again, rather than a breath, a color, a movement? That I do not ache to touch thee once again, and to feel once again thy touch upon my body? Thou knowest all that I might say, but no one god possesses all powers. I should not complain, but I fear, my lord, I fear the madness that sometimes comes upon me: Never to sleep, never to eat, never to touch a solid thing. How long has it been . . . ?"

"Many centuries."

". . . And I know that all wives be bitches unto their lords, and I ask of thee thy forgiveness. But to whom else may I address my bitching, but to thee?"

"Well taken, my Nephytha. Would that I could embody thee once more, for I, too, am lonely. Thou knowest I have tried."

"Yes."

"When thou hast broken the Thing That Cries, then wilt thou discipline Osiris and Anubis?"

"Of course."

"Please do not destroy them immediately, if they can help me. Grant them some measure of mercy if they will give me back to you."

"Perhaps."

". . . For I am so lonely. I wish that I could go away from here."

"You require a place surrounded by water, to keep you alive. You require an entire world, to keep you occupied."

"I know. I know. . . ."

"If Osiris had not been so deadly set upon vengeance, things might have been different. Now, thou knowest, I am bound to slay him when I have resolved the matter of the Nameless."

"Yes, I know, and I agree. But what of Anubis?"

"Periodically, he attempts to slay me, which is of no great import. Mayhap, I shall forgive him. But not my bird-headed Angel, never."

The Prince Who Had Been A King (among other things) seats himself upon a rock and stares out across the waters and then upward into the bottom of the sea. The lights stir lazily above him. High mountaintops poke with their peaks into the bottommost depths. The light is pale and diffuse, seeming to come from all directions. The Prince tosses a flat stone so that it skips out upon the waves that are before him, away.

"Tell me again of the days of the battle, a millennium ago," she says, "of the days when he fell, who was your son and your father, the mightiest warrior ever raised up to fight for the six races of man."

The Prince is silent, staring out across the waters.

"Why?" he asks.

"Because each time that you tell it, you are moved to undertake some new action."

". . . And to meet with some new failure," finishes the Prince.

"Tell me," she says.

The Prince sighs, and the heavens roar above him, where swim the bright fish with transparent bellies. He holds forth his hand, and a stone skips back into it from out the sea. The wind passes and returns, caressing him.

He begins to speak.

Angel of
the House of Fire

Upward stares Anubis, seeing death.

Death is a black horse shadow without a horse to cast it.

Anubis stares, gripping his staff with both hands.

"Hail, Anubis, Angel of the House of the Dead," comes a voice rich and resonant that sings through the great Hall.

"Hail," says Anubis, softly, "Master of the House of Fire—which is no more."

"This place is changed somewhat."

"It has been a long time," says Anubis.

"Quite."

"May I inquire as to the state of your health these days?"

"I find it to be quite stable, as always."

"May I inquire as to what brings you here?"

"Yes. You may."

There is a pause.

"I had thought you dead," says Anubis.

"I know."

"I am pleased that you survived, somehow, that deadly on-slaught."

"Likewise. It has taken me many centuries to return from the place unto which I was cast subsequent to that foolish use of the Hammer. I had retreated beyond space as you know it a moment before Osiris struck with the blow which smashes suns. It drove me further than I intended to go, into the places that are not places."

"And what have you been doing all this time?"

"Coming back."

"You alone, Typhon, of all the gods, could have survived that fiery falling."

"What are you trying to say?"

"Set the Destroyer, your father, died in that battle."

"Aieee!"

Anubis covers his ears and closes his eyes, letting his staff fall to the floor. The cry that rings through the Hall is a soulsearing thing, half human, half animal, and it hurts to hear even that portion of it which he does.

After a time, there is a mighty silence, and Anubis opens his eyes and lowers his hands. The shadow is smaller now, and nearer.

"I take it that the Nameless was also destroyed at that time?"

"I do not know."

"Then what of your master, Thoth?"

"He abdicated as Lord of Life and Death, and retreated beyond the Middle Worlds."

"I find that difficult to believe."

Anubis shrugs.

"It is a fact of life, and of death."

"Why should he do such a thing?"

"I do not know."

"I wish to go to him. Where may he be found?"

"I do not know."

"You are not very helpful, Angel. Tell me, now, who is running things in the absence of my brother, your master?"

"I do not understand what you mean."

"Come now, dog-face, you have lived long enough to appreciate a simple question. Who controls the tides of the Power?"

"The House of Life and the House of the Dead, of course."

"Of course, indeed! And who is the House of Life these days?"

"Osiris, naturally."

"I see. . . ."

The shadow rears again, grows larger.

"Dog-face," says Typhon, the shadow of a horse rampant, "I suspect conspiracy—but I never slay on the basis of suspicion alone. I feel, though, that all is not right. I've a dead father who may need avenging—and if my brother has been wronged, then blood shall burn for this, also. You had need to answer me quickly and without much forethought. You may have said more than you intended. Now hear me: Of all things, I know that you fear me most. You have always been afraid of the shadow of a horse, and for good reason. If this shadow falls upon you, Angel, you shall cease to exist. Utterly. And it will fall upon you, if you had aught to do with those things of which I disapprove. Do I make myself clear?"

"Yes, mighty Typhon. Thou art the only god whom I worship."

Then springs Anubis, with a howl, a glowing bridle suddenly in his right hand.

The shadow of a hoof passes near him and he falls to the floor. The shadow falls upon the sparkling, silver bridle and it vanishes.

"Anubis, you are a fool! Why did you seek to bind me?"

"Because thou hast made me to fear for my life, Lord!"

"Do not arise! Do not move a muscle, else you shall pass into nothingness! The only reason you could fear me is if you bear a burden of guilt."

"This is not so! I fear that thou mayst misinterpret and choose to strike on that basis. I do not wish to pass into nothingness. I sought to bind thee in self-defense, that I might hold thee until thou hast all the facts. For I confess that my position makes me to look guilty upon the face of things."

The shadow moves and falls upon Anubis' outstretched right arm. The arm withers and goes limp.

"You will never replace that arm which was raised against me, Jackal! Graft on a new one and it, too, will wither. Put there an arm out of metal and it will refuse to function. I leave you only a left hand for your mischief. I shall find the facts— *all* the facts—myself. If you bear the guilt I now think you to bear, I will be judge, jury and executioner. No bridle of silver nor reins of gold can stay Typhon, know that. And know that if my entire shadow pass over you, not even dust will remain. I will return to the House of the Dead one day soon, and, if aught be askew, a new cur shall rule here."

Fire begins at the edges of the black silhouette. It rears as if to strike once more, the flames flash bright, and Anubis is alone on the floor of the great Hall.

He stands slowly and retrieves his staff with his left hand. His tongue darts forth redly, and he staggers to his throne. A great window appears in the middle of the air, and he regards the Lord of Life through it.

"Osiris!" he says. "The Devil lives!"

"What mean you?" comes the reply.

"Tonight, there was the shadow of a horse come upon me."

"This is not good. Especially when you have sent forth a new emissary."

"How do you know this?"

"I have my ways. But I, too, have done this thing—for the first time—and it is my son, Horus. Hope that I can recall him in time."

"Yes. I've always had a liking for Horus."

"And what of your emissary?"

"I shall not recall him. I should like very much to see Typhon attempt *his* destruction."

"Your Wakim—who is he, really? Who was he?"

"That is my affair."

"If—somehow—he is the one I think he may be—and you know who I mean—call him off, dog, or there shall never be peace between us, if both of us survive."

Anubis chuckles.

"Was there ever?"

"No," says Osiris, "since we're being candid."

"But the Prince has actually threatened us, for the first time, threathened to end our reign."

"Yes, this twelve-year past—and we must act. We've centuries, he's indicated, ere he'll move. But move he will, for he always keeps his word. Who knows, though, what he has in mind?"

"Not I."

"What has happened to your right arm?"

"The shadow fell upon it."

"And we shall both of us go in this manner, beneath the shadow, if you do not recall your emissary. Typhon has changed the picture completely. We must contact the Prince—seek to bargain with him, to placate him."

"He is too clever to be deceived by false promises, and you underestimate Wakim."

"Perhaps we should bargain in good faith—not to restore him, of course. . . ."

"No! We shall triumph!"

"Prove it by replacing your arm with one that will work!"

"I shall."

"Good-bye, Anubis, and remember—not even the fugue works against the Angel of the House of Fire."

"I know. Good-bye, Angel of the House of Life."

"Why do you use my ancient title?"

"Because of your unbecoming fear that the old days are upon us once more, Osiris."

"Then call off Wakim."

"No."

"Then good-bye, foolish Angel, most fallen."

"Adieu."

And the window is full of stars and power until it is closed, with a left-handed movement between the flames.

There is silence in the House of the Dead.

Sketches

... **A**n eunuch priest of the highest caste sets tapers before a pair of old shoes.

... The dog worries the dirty glove which hath seen many better centuries.

... The blind Norns strike a tiny silver anvil with fingers that are mallets. Upon the metal lies a length of blue light.

The Coming of
the Steel General

Upward stares Wakim, seeing the Steel General.

"Faintly do I feel that I should have knowledge of him," says Wakim.

"Come now!" says Vramin, his eyes and cane flashing fires green. "All know of the General, who ranges alone. Out of the pages of history come the thundering hoofbeats of his war horse Bronze. He flew with the Lafayette Escadrille. He fought in the delaying action at Jarama Valley. He helped to hold Stalingrad in the dead of winter. With a handful of friends, he tried to invade Cuba. On every battleground, he has left a portion of himself. He camped out in Washington when times were bad, until a greater General asked him to go away. He was beaten in Little Rock, had acid thrown in his face in Berkeley. He was put on the Attorney General's list, because he had once been a member of the I.W.W. All the causes for which he has fought are now dead, but a part of him died also as each was born and carried to its fruition. He survived, somehow, his

century, with artificial limbs and artificial heart and veins, with
false teeth and a glass eye, with a plate in his skull and bones
out of plastic, with pieces of wire and porcelain inside him—
until finally science came to make these things better than
those with which man is normally endowed. He was again replaced, piece by piece, until, in the following century, he was
far superior to any man of flesh and blood. And so again he
fought the rebel battle, being smashed over and over again in
the wars the colonies fought against the mother planet, and in
the wars the individual worlds fought against the Federation.
He is always on *some* Attorney General's list, and he plays his
banjo and he does not care, for he has placed himself beyond
the law by always obeying its spirit rather than its letter. He has
had his metal replaced with flesh on many occasions and been
a full man once more—but always he hearkens to some distant
bugle and plays his banjo and follows—and then he loses his
humanity again. He shot craps with Leon Trotsky, who taught
him that writers are underpaid; he shared a boxcar with Woody
Guthrie, who taught him his music and that singers are underpaid; he supported Fidel Castro for a time, and learned that
lawyers are underpaid. He is almost invariably beaten and
used and taken advantage of, and he does not care, for his ide-
als mean more to him than his flesh. Now, of course, the
Prince Who Was A Thousand is an unpopular cause. I take it,
from what you say, that those who would oppose the House
of Life and the House of the Dead will be deemed supporters of
the Prince, who has solicited no support—not that that matters. And I daresay you oppose the Prince, Wakim. I should
also venture a guess that the General will support him, inas-
much as the Prince is a minority group all by himself. The
General may be beaten, but he can never be destroyed, Wakim.
Here he is now. Ask him yourself, if you'd like."

The Steel General, who has dismounted, stands now before

Wakim and Vramin like an iron statue at ten o'clock on a summer evening with no moon.

"I have seen your beacon, Angel of the Seventh Station."

"Alas, but the title perished with the Station, sir."

"I still recognize the rights of the government in exile," says the General, and his voice is a thing of such beauty that one could listen to it for years.

"Thank you. But I fear that you have come too late. This one—this Wakim—who is a master of temporal fugue, would, I feel, destroy the Prince and thus remove any basis for our return. Is that not so, Wakim?"

"Of course."

". . . Unless we might find a champion." says Vramin.

"You need look no further," says the General. "It is best you yield to me now, Wakim. I say this with no malice."

"And I reply with no malice: Go to hell. If every bit of you were to be destroyed, then I feel there would no longer be a Steel General—and there would never be again. I think a rebel such as yourself deserves annihilation, and I am here."

"Many have thought so, and I am still waiting."

"Then wait no longer," says Wakim, and he moves forward. "The time is here, and begging to be filled."

Then Vramin encircles Madrak and himself with green fires, and they look upon the facing of the masters.

At this moment Bronze rears, and six diamonds flash among the colors of Blis.

The Town Scrier
of Liglamenti

Horus has entered the Middle Worlds, and he comes to the world of mists that is called D'donori by its inhabitants, meaning Place of Contentment. As he disembarks from his chariot that has crossed the cold and airless night he hears the sounds of armed strife about him within the great mists that cover over all of D'donori.

Slaying with his hands the three knights who fall upon him, he comes at length to the high walls of the city of Liglamenti, whose rulers have in the past had some reason to consider him a god kindly disposed toward their welfare.

D'donori is a world which, though it lies within the tides of the Power, has never been subject to the plagues, the wars, the famines that limit the populations of the other Midworlds. This is because the inhabitants of D'donori take care of their own problems. D'donori is made up of numerous small city-states and duchies which are constantly at war with one another, uniting only for purposes of destroying anyone who attempts to unite them on a permanent basis.

Horus approaches the great gates of Liglamenti and bangs upon them with his fist. The booming sound carries throughout the city and the gates creak upon their hinges.

A guard hurls down a torch through the gloom and follows it with an arrow which, of course, misses its mark—for Horus is able to know the thoughts of his attacker and mark the line of the arrow's flight. He steps to the side as the arrow whizzes past him and he stands in the light of the torch.

"Open your gates or I'll unhinge them!" he calls out.

"Who are you that walks about weaponless, wearing only a loincloth, and would give me orders?"

"I am Horus."

"I do not believe you."

"You have less than a minute to live," says Horus, "unless you open these gates to me. Your death will be the proof that Horus does not lie. I will then unhinge these gates and enter here, walking upon you as I pass in search of your Lord."

"Wait! If truly thou beest he, understand that I am only doing my duty and following orders of my Lord. Do not think me blasphemous if I should refuse admittance to any who may call himself Horus. How do I know but that thou art an enemy who would say this to deceive me?"

"Would an enemy dare to be so foolish?"

"Mayhap. For most men are fools."

Horus shrugs and raises his fist once more. A vibrant musical note stirs then within the air, and the gates of Liglamenti shiver upon their hinges and the guard within his armor.

Horus has increased in stature by now, to near three meters. His breechclout is the color of blood. The torch flickers at his feet. He draws back his fist.

"Wait! I will give thee entrance!"

Horus lowers his fist and the music dies. His height decreases by a third.

The guard causes the portal to be opened and Horus enters Liglamenti.

Coming at length to the fog-shrouded palace of its ruler, the Lord Dilwit, Duke of Ligla, Horus learns that word of his arrival has preceded him from the walls. The somber, black-bearded Duke, whose crown has been grafted upon his scalp, manages as much of a smile as he is able; that is, the showing of a double row of teeth between tight-drawn lips. He nods, slightly.

"Thou art truly Horus?" he asks.

"Yes."

"It is told that every time the god Horus passes this way there is difficulty in recognizing him."

"And no wonder," says Horus. "In all this fog it is rather miraculous that you manage to recognize one another."

Dilwit snorts his equivalent of a laugh. "True—often we do not, and slay our own men in error. But each time Horus has come, the ruling Lord has provided a test. The last time. . . ."

". . . The last time, for Lord Bulwah, I sent a wooden arrow into a two-foot cube of marble so that either end protruded from a side."

"Thou rememberest!"

"Of course. I am Horus. Do you still have that cube?"

"Yes. Certainly."

"Then take me to it now."

They enter the torchlit throne room, where the shaggy pelts of predators offer the eye its only diversion from the glittering war weapons upon the walls. Set atop a small pedestal in a recessed place to the left of the throne is a cube of gray and orange marble which contains an arrow.

"There you see it," says Dilwit, gesturing.

Horus approaches, regards the display.

"I'll design my own test this time," says he. "I'll fetch you back the arrow."

"It might be drawn. That is no—"

Horus raises his right fist to shoulder level, swings it forward and down, striking the stone, which shatters. He retrieves the arrow and hands it to Dilwit.

"I am Horus," he states.

Dilwit regards the arrow, the gravel, the chunks of marble.

"Thou art indeed Horus," he agrees. "What may I do for thee?"

"D'donori has always been justly famous for its scriers. Those of Liglamenti have oft been exceeding good. Therefore, I would consult with your chief scrier, as I've several questions I'd have answered."

"This would be old Freydag," says Dilwit, flicking rock dust from his red and green kilt. "He is indeed one of the great ones, but . . ."

"But what?" asks Horus, already reading Dilwit's thought, but waiting politely, nevertheless.

"He is, Great Horus, a mighty reader of entrails, and none but those of the human sort will serve him. Now, we seldom keep prisoners, as this can run into some expense—and volunteers are even harder to come by, for things such as this."

"Could not Freydag be persuaded to make do with the entrails of some animal, for this one occasion?"

Horus reads again and sighs.

"Of course, Great Horus. But he will not guarantee the same level of reception as he would with better components."

"I wonder why this should be?"

"I cannot answer this, Most Potent Horus, being no scrier myself—though my mother and sister both had the Sight—but of all scriers, I know scatologists to be the queerest sort. Take Freydag, now. He's quite nearsighted, he says, and this means—"

"Furnish him with the necessary components, and advise me when he is ready to entertain my questions!" says Horus.

"Yes, Puissant Horus. I will organize a raiding party immediately, as I can see thou art anxious."

"Most anxious."

". . . And I've a neighbor could use a lesson in observing boundaries!"

Dilwit springs upon his throne, and reaching upward takes down the long gol-horn which hangs above it. Three times does he place it to his lips and blow until his cheeks bulge and redden and his eyes start forth from beneath the pelt of his brows. Then does he replace the horn, sway, and collapse upon his ducal seat.

"My chieftains will attend me momently," he gasps.

Momently, there comes the sound of hoofbeats, and three kilted warriors, mounted upon the unicornlike golindi, come riding, riding, riding, into and about the chamber, staying only when Dilwit raises his hand and cries out, "A raid! A raid, my hearties! Upon Uiskeagh the Red. Half a dozen captives I'll have of him, ere the mist lightens with tomorrow's dawn!"

"Captives, did you say, Lord?" calls out the one in black and tan.

"You heard me right."

"Before tomorrow's dawn!" A spear is raised.

Two more flash high.

"Before tomorrow's dawn!"

"Aye!"

And they circle the chamber and depart.

The following dawn, Horus is awakened and conducted to the room where six naked men lie, hands and ankles bound together behind their backs, their bodies covered with gashes and welts. This chamber is small, cold, lighted by four torches; its one window opens upon a wall of fog. Many sheets of that monthly journal the Ligla *Times* are spread upon the floor, covering it fully. Leaning against the window sill, a short, age-tonsured man, pink-faced, hollow-cheeked and squinting, sharpens several brief blades with a whetting bar. He wears a white apron and a half-furnished smile. His pale eyes move upon Horus and he nods several times.

"I understand thou hast some questions," he says, pausing to gasp between several words.

"You understand correctly. I've three."

"Only three, Holy Horus? That means one set of entrails will doubtless do for all. Surely, a god as wise as thyself could think of more questions. Since we have the necessary materials it is a shame to waste them. It's been so long. . . ."

"Three, nevertheless, are all the questions I have for the entrail-oracle."

"Very well, then," sighs Freydag. "In that case, we shall use his," and he indicates with his blade one gray-bearded man whose dark eyes are fixed upon his own. "Boltag is the name."

"You know him?"

"He is a distant cousin of mine. Also, he is the Lord Uiskeagh's chief scrier—a charlatan, of course. It is good fortune that has finally delivered him into my hands."

The one called Boltag spits upon the *Times* obituary section when this is spoken. "Thou are the fraud, oh mighty misreader of innards!" says he.

"Liar!" cries Freydag, scrambling to his side and seizing him by the beard. "This ends thy infamous career!" and he slits the other's belly. Reaching in, he draws forth a handful of entrails and spreads them upon the floor. Boltag cries, moans, lies still. Freytag slashes along the bending length of the intestines, spreading their contents with his fingers. He crouches low and leans far forward. "Now, what be thy questions, son of Osiris?" he inquires.

"First," says Horus, "where may I find the Prince Who Was A Thousand? Second, who is the emissary of Anubis? Third, where is *he* now?"

Freytag mumbles and prods at the steaming stuff upon the floor. Boltag moans once again and stirs.

Horus attempts to read the thoughts of the scrier, but they tumble about so that finally it is as if he were staring out the room's one window.

Then Freydag speaks:

"In the Citadel of Marachek," he says, "at Midworlds' Center, there shalt thou meet with one who can take thee into the presence thou seekest."

". . . Strangely," mutters Boltag, gesturing with his head, "thou hast read that part aright. But thy failing vision—was clouded—by that bit of mesentery thou hast erroneously mixed—into things. . . ." With a mighty effort Boltag rolls nearer, gasps, "And thou—dost not tell—Great Horus—that he will meet with mighty peril—and, ultimately—failure. . . ."

"Silence!" cries Freydag. "I did not call thee in for a consultation!"

"They are my innards! I will not have them misread by a poseur!"

"The next two answers are not yet come clear, dear Horus," says Freydag, slashing at another length of entrail.

"False seer!" sobs Boltag. "Marachek will also lead him to the emissary of Anubis—whose name is spelt out in my blood—there—on the editorial page! That name—being—Wakim. . . ."

"Oh false!" cries Freydag, slashing further.

"Hold!" says Horus, his hand falling upon the man's shoulder. "Your colleague speaks truly in one respect, for I know his present name to be Wakim."

Freydag pauses, considers the editorial page.

"Amen," he agrees. "Even an amateur may suffer an occasional flash of insight."

". . . So it seems I am destined to meet with Wakim after all, if I go to the place called Marachek—and go there I must. But as to my second question: Beyond the name of Wakim, I wish to know his true identity. Who was he before Lord Anubis renamed him and sent him forth from the House of the Dead?"

Freydag moves his head nearer the floor, stirs the stuff before him, hacks at another length.

"This thing, Glorious Horus, is hidden from me. The oracle will not reveal it—"

"Dotard . . . !" gasps Boltag. ". . . It is there, so—plain—to see. . . ."

Horus reaches after the gutless seer's dying thought, and the hackles rise upon his neck as he pursues it. But no fearsome name is framed within his mind, for the other has expired.

Horus covers his eyes and shudders, as a thing so very near to the edge of comprehension suddenly fades away and is gone.

When Horus lowers his hand, Freydag is standing once more and smiling down upon his cousin's corpse.

"Mountebank!" he says, sniffing, and wipes his hands upon his apron.

A strange, small, beastly shadow stirs upon the wall.

Arms and the Steel Man

Diamond hooves striking the ground, rising, falling again. Rising . . .

Wakim and the Steel General face one another, unmoving.

A minute goes by, then three, and now the falling hooves of the beast called Bronze come down with a sound like thunder upon the fairground of Blis, for, each time that they strike, the force of their falling is doubled.

It is said that a fugue battle is actually settled in these first racking moments of regard, before the initial temporal phase is executed, in these moments which will be wiped from the face of Time by the outcome of the striving, never to have actually existed.

The ground shakes now as Bronze strikes it, and blue fires come forth from his nostrils, burning downward into Blis.

Wakim glistens with perspiration now; and the Steel General's finger twitches, the one upon which he wears his humanity-ring.

Eleven minutes pass.

Wakim vanishes.

The Steel General vanishes.

Bronze descends again, and tents fall down, buildings shatter, cracks appear within the ground.

Thirty seconds ago, Wakim is standing behind the General and Wakim is standing before the General, and the Wakim who stands behind, who has just arrived in that instant, clasps his hands together and raises them for a mighty blow upon that metal helm—

—while thirty-five seconds ago, the Steel General appears behind the Wakim of that moment of Time, draws back his hand and swings it—

—while the Wakim of thirty seconds ago, seeing himself in fugue, delivering his two-handed blow, is released to vanish, which he does, into a time ten seconds before, when he prepares to emulate his future image observed—

—as the General of thirty-five seconds before the point of attack sees himself draw back his hand, and vanishes to a time twelve seconds previously. . . .

All of these, because a foreguard in Time is necessary to preserve one's future existence . . .

. . . And a rearguard, one's back . . .

. . . While all the while, somewhere/when/perhaps, now, Bronze is rearing and descending, and a probable city trembles upon its foundation.

. . . And the Wakim of forty seconds before the point of attack, seeing his arrival, departs twenty seconds backward—one minute of probable time therefore being blurred by the fugue battle, and so subject to alteration.

. . . The General of forty-seven seconds before the point of attack retreats fifteen to strike again, as his self of that moment observes him and drops back eight—

. . . The Wakim of one minute before goes back ten seconds—

Fugue!

Wakim behind the Steel General, attacking, at minus seventy seconds sees the General behind Wakim, attacking, as both see him and his other see both.

All four vanish, at a pace of eleven, fifteen, nineteen and twenty-five seconds.

... And all the while, somewhere/when/perhaps, Bronze rears, falls, and shock waves go forth.

The point of initial encounter draws on, as General before General and Wakim before Wakim face and fugue.

Five minutes and seven seconds of the future stand in abeyance as twelve Generals and nine Wakims look upon one another.

... Five minutes and twenty-one seconds, as nineteen Wakims and fourteen Generals glare in frozen striking-stances.

... Eight minutes and sixteen seconds before the point of attack, one hundred twenty-three Wakims and one hundred thirty-one Generals assess one another and decide upon the moment . . .

... To attack *en masse*, within that instant of time, leaving their past selves to shift for themselves in defense—perhaps, if this instant be the wrong one, to fall, and so end this encounter, also. But things must end somewhere. Depending upon the lightning calculations and guesses, each has picked this point as the best for purposes of determining the future and holding the focus. And as the armies of Wakims and the General clash together, the ground begins to rumble beneath their feet and the fabric of Time itself protests this use which has been made of its dispositions. A wind begins to blow and things become unreal about them, wavering between being and becoming and after-being. And somewhere Bronze smashes his diamonds into the continent and spews forth gouts of blue fire upon it. Corpses of bloodied and broken Wakims and fragments of shattered Generals drift through the twisting places beyond the focus of their struggles and are buffeted by the winds. These be the dead of probability, for there can be no past slaying now, and the future is being remade. The focus of the fugue has become this moment of intensity, and they clash with a force that sends widening ripples of change outward through the universe, rising, diminishing, gone by, as Time once more tricks history around events.

Beyond their midst, Bronze descends and somewhere a city begins to come apart. The poet raises his cane, but its green fires cannot cancel the blue flare that Bronze exhales now like a fountain upon the world. Now there are only nine cities on Blis and Time is burning them down. Buildings, machines, corpses, babies, pavilions, these are taken by the wind from the flame, and they pass, wavering, by the fairground. Regard their colors. Red? There's a riverbank, green stream hung above, and flying purple rocks. Yellow and gray and black the city beneath the three lime-hued bridges. Now the creamy sea is the sky and buzzsaw come the breezes. The odors of Blis are smoke and charred flesh. The sounds are screams amid the clashing of broken gears and the rapid-fire rainfall of running feet like guilt within the Black Daddy Night that comes on like unconsciousness now.

"Cease!" cries Vramin, becoming a blazing green giant in the midst of chaos. "You will lay waste the entire world if you continue!" he cries, and his voice comes down like thunder and whistles and trumpets upon them.

They continue to strive, however, and the magician takes his friend Madrak by the arm and attempts to open them a gateway of escape from Blis.

"Civilians are dying!" cries a moment of the General.

A moment of Wakim laughs.

"What difference does a uniform make in the House of the Dead?"

A great green door appears in outline, grows more substantial, begins to open.

Vramin diminishes in size. As the door swings wide, he and Madrak are both swept toward it, as tall waves race and topple upon a wind-slashed ocean.

The armies of Wakim and the General are also raised by the waves of chaos and driven by the winds of change until they, too, are come at last to the green gateway which stands now wide, like a luminous magnet/drain/whirlpool's center. Still striving, they flow toward it, and one by one pass within and are gone.

Bronze begins to move very slowly as the gateway closes, but somehow passes through it before the chaos comes upon the empty space it occupied.

Then the roaring and the movement cease, and the entire world of Blis seems to sigh within the moment of its reprieve. Many things are broken and people dead or dying at this moment, which could have been one set thirty-three seconds before Wakim and the General began the fugue which will not now begin upon the litter-strewn fairground with its crevasses and its steaming craters.

Among the fallen archways, the toppled towers, the flattened buildings, salvation strides with its sword of fires unsheathed. The fevers of the day come forth from the Houses of Power, and somewhere a dog is barking.

Wrath of the Red Lady

Megra of Kalgan flees, half unseeing now, through the many-formed shapes of the crowd. As she moves, there comes up a new screaming, from out many throats. A cold, wild wind begins to blow among the colors and shapes of the fairground. Looking upward, she sees a sight that holds her eyes upon it and causes her feet to falter, there amid the buffeted tents and the flapping pennons.

It is the Steel General on the back of Bronze, riding. Downward he comes, slowing, slowing. She has read of him, heard of him, for he exists in the apocalyptic writings of all nations and peoples.

Behind her, a pavilion goes up in a burst of green flame. Now, as she watches, a green flare cuts the air, hovers, burns there.

The great beast Bronze changes his course, slowing, still slowing with each stride, as he descends upon the ruined pavilion where she had left Wakim and Madrak the warrior-priest to their combat. She looks back in that direction, but her height, within any crowd, prevents her seeing beyond whatever walls of humanity may be standing near.

Finally, the Steel General himself is lost to her sight, and she continues to push her way through the many-footed mass and toward the latest tent of death.

She calls upon her strength now to force a path where others would be left standing: she moves like a swimmer doing a breast stroke amid bodies large and many-limbed, machines with faces and feathers, women with blinking lights within their breasts, men with spurs at their joints, hordes of ordinary-appearing persons of the six races, a woman from whose blue thorax violin notes constantly emerge, coming now in a frantic crescendo which it hurts her ears to hear, and passes then by a man who carries his heart within a humming casket close against his side; she strikes a creature like an uncovered umbrella, which encircles her with a tentacle in its frenzy; now she pushes past a horde of pimply green dwarves, turns up an alleyway between pavilions, crosses an open place where the ground is hard-packed, caked with sawdust and straw; she moves between two more pavilions as a gradual diminishing of light begins to occur about her, and she strikes at a small flying thing which circles and gibbers around her head.

She turns then and regards a sight that is like nothing she has ever seen before.

There is a red chariot standing, with empty traces, still smoldering with the dust of the sky. Its wheels have dug deep ruts into the ground for a distance of perhaps three meters. Beyond that, there is no track.

Within the chariot stands the cloaked and veiled figure of a tall woman. A lock of her hair hangs down, the color of blood. Her right hand, almost as red as its nails, holds reins which are attached to nothing before the chariot. The flying, gibbering thing at which Megra had struck stands now upon this woman's shoulder, its leathery wings folded and invisible, its hairless tail twitching.

"Megra of Kalgan," says a voice that strikes her like a jeweled glove, "you have come to me as I wished," and the vapors that rise from the chariot swirl about the red women.

Megra shivers then, feeling a thing that is like a piece of the black ice that lies between the stars, touch upon her heart.

"Who are you?" she asks.

"I am called Isis, Mother of Dust."

"And why do you seek me? I do not know you, Lady—save by reputation out of legend."

Isis laughs and Megra reaches out and touches a metal strut that bolsters the pavilion to her right.

"I seek you, little rabbit, that I might wreak a terrible thing upon you."

"Why, Lady? I have done nothing to you."

"Perhaps, and perhaps not. I may be wrong, though I think not. I shall know shortly, however. We must wait."

"For what?"

"The conduct of the battle which I believe is about to occur."

"As much as I enjoy your company, I am not about to wait here, for any purpose. You must excuse me. I've an errand—"

". . . Of mercy! I know—" and she laughs once more, and Megra's grip tightens upon the metal strut so that it buckles within her hand and she tears it free of the pavilion, causing it to sway and creak, there at her right.

The laughter of Isis dies upon the air.

"Impertinent child! You would take up arms against me?"

"If necessary, though I doubt I'll need them, Madam."

"Then be frozen like a statue where you stand!" and as she speaks, the Red Witch touches a ruby pendant at her throat and a ray of light speeds forth from its heart and falls upon Megra.

Striving against a numbing paralysis which comes then over her, Megra hurls the metal strut toward Isis. It spins like a great gray wheel, a saw blade, a discus, as it falls toward the chariot.

Dropping the reins and raising an arm, Isis continues to clutch her pendant, from which more rays now leap forth. These fall upon the turning metal which for an instant blazes like a meteor and vanishes, a heap of slag falling to the baked ground beneath its place of combustion.

During this time, Megra feels herself released from the icy grip that had seized her, and she leaps toward the chariot, striking it with her shoulder, so that Isis is thrown to the ground and her familiar scoots, chittering, behind a swaying wheel.

Megra steps to her side, ready to strike her with the flat of her hand, and seeing that her veil has fallen, hesitates for an instant to touch a thing of such beauty as she beholds—of eyes dark and large within an heart-shaped face, so red and blazing with life, and lashes that reach to the brows with a movement like the wings of crimson butterflies, and teeth pink as flesh within a sudden smile of the sort that may sometimes be seen when staring into flames.

The darkness continues to deepen and the wind grows more wild, and suddenly the ground is shaken, as with some distant blow.

The light of the pendant touches Megra once more, and Isis attempts to stand, falls to her knees, frowns.

"Oh little child, what fate awaits you!" she says, and Megra, remembering the legends out of the old days, prays not only to an official god of the established religion, but to one who fell long ago, saying, "Osiris, Lord of Life, deliver me from the wrath of thy consort! But if thou wilt not hear my prayer. I then address my words to the dark god, Set, both beloved of and feared by this Lady. Save my life!" And then her voice goes still within her throat. Standing now, Isis looks about her, as the ground is shaken and shaken again by a terrible pounding, and noonday is become dusk within the heavens and over the land. There is a blue glow come up in the distance now, and somewhere a sound as of the clashing of two armies. There are shouts, shrieks and wailings. The prospect begins to sway in the distance, as though the world lies beneath heat waves.

"You may think this to be your deliverance," cries Isis, "an answer to your blasphemous mouthings! But you are wrong! I know that I must not slay you now, but do a thing far more fearsome. I shall give you a gift that is all unhuman wisdom and human shame. For I have learned what I came to Blis to discover, and vengeance must be had! —Come with me now, into my chariot! Quickly! This world may soon cease to exist— for the General is not defeating your lover! Damn him!"

Stiffly, slowly, Megra's muscles obey the command, and she mounts the chariot. The Red Witch comes and stands beside her, adjusts her veil. In the distance, a green giant is screaming into the wind words which cannot be heard. Flickering fragments of everything seem to be spinning around within a great vortex that moves about the fairground. Everything blurs, doubles, triples, some images shattering, others remaining. Cracks and crevasses appear within the ground. In the distance, a city is falling. The little familiar hides within the witch's cloak, a cry upon its lips. The dusk is broken now and the night comes down like thunder, and colors all splash together in the dark places where there should be no colors. Isis raises the reins and red flames leap up within the chariot, burning nothing, but encasing them within the heart of a ruby or the egg of the phoenix, and there is no sense of movement nor sound of passage, nor any other sound, suddenly, but now the world called Blis with its trouble, with its chaos and its plague, its salvation, lies far away from them, like the bright mouth of a well down which they are rushing, stars like spittle splashing beside.

The Thing That
Cries in the Night

In the days when I reigned
as Lord of Life and Death,
      says the Prince Who Was A Thousand,
in those days, at Man's request,
did I lay the Middle Worlds within a sea of power,
tidal, turning thing,
thing to work with peaceful sea change
the birth,
growth,
death
designs upon them;

then all this gave
to Angels ministrant,
their Stations bordering Midworlds,
their hands to stir the tides.
And for many ages did we rule so,
elaborating the life,

tempering the death,
promoting the growth,
extending
the shores of that great, great sea,
as more and more of the Outworlds
were washed by the curling,
crowned by creation's foam.

Then one day,
brooding on the vast abyss
of such a world, brave,
good-seeming,
though dead, barren,
not then touched by the life,
       I roused some sleeping thing
with the kiss of the tide I rode.

And I feared that thing which awakened,
issued forth,
attacked me—
came out the bowels of the land—
sought to destroy me:
thing which devoured the life of the planet,
slept for a season within it,
then hungry rose and vicious sought.
Feeding upon the tides of the Life,
it awakened.
It touched upon thee, my wife,
and I may not restore thy body,
though I preserved this breath of thee.

It drank, as a man drinks wine,
of the Life;
and every weapon in my arsenal

was discharged upon it,
but it did not die,
did not lapse into quiescence.
Rather, it tried to depart.

I contained it.
Diverting the power of my Stations,
I set up the field,
field of neutral energies
caging the whole of the world.

Were it able to travel the places of Life,
devastate an entire world,
it must need be destroyed.

I tried, I failed—
many tried, many failed—
during the century's half
I held it prisoner
upon that nameless world.

Then were the Midworlds cast into chaos,
for want of my control
over the life the death the growth.
Great was my pain.
New Stations were a building, but all too slow.

It was mine to lay the field once more,
but I might not free the Nameless.
I held not the power
to keep my shadow prisoner
and hold the Worlds of Life.
Now, among my Angels

grew up dissension's stalk.
Quickly did I harvest it—
the price being some loyalty,
as even then I knew.

You, my Nephytha,
did not approve when my father,
risking the wrath of the Angel Osiris,
returned from Midworld's end,
to undertake the ultimate love
that is destruction.
You did not approve,
because my father Set,
mightiest warrior who ever lived,
was also our son in those days gone by,
our son, those days in Marachek,
after I had broken the temporal barrier,
to live once again through all time,
for the wisdom that is Past.

I did not know that, as time came back,
I would come to father the one who had been my father,
sun-eyed Set,
Wielder of the Star Wand,
Wearer of the Gauntlet,
Strider over Mountains.

You did not approve,
but you did not gainsay this battle,
and Set girded himself for the struggle.

Now, Set had never been defeated.
There was nothing he would not undertake to conquer.

He knew that the Steel General had been broken
        and scattered by the Nameless.
But he was not afraid.

Holding forth his right hand,
he drew upon it the Gauntlet of Power,
which instantly grew
to cover over his body,
that but the brightness of his eyes shone through.

He placed upon his feet
the boots
which permitted him
to straddle the air and the water.
Then, with a black strand
he hung about his waist the sheath of the Star Wand,
ultimate weapon,
born of the blind smiths of Norn,
which only he might wield.
No, he was not afraid.

Ready then was he to depart my circling fortress,
descend upon the world,
where the Nameless crept,
spread,
swirled,
furious and hungry.
Then did his other son, my brother Typhon,
black shadow out of the void,
appear,
begging to go in his place.

But Set did deny him this thing,
opened the hatch,

pushed himself into darkness,
fell toward the face of the world.

Now, for three hundred hours did they battle,
over two weeks by the Old Reckoning,
before the Nameless began to weaken.
Set pushed the attack,
hurt the Thing,
prepared the blow of death.

He had fought it on the waters of the oceans
        under the oceans,
had fought it on dry land,
in the air's cold center,
and on the tops of mountains.
He had pursued it about the globe,
awaiting the opening that would permit
        the final thrust.

The force of their conflict shattered two continents,
made the oceans to boil,
filled the air with clouds.

The rocks split and melted,
the heavens were laced with sonic booms
like invisible jewels of the fog,
the steam.

A dozen times did I restrain Typhon,
who would go to his aid.
Then, as the Nameless coiled and reared
to a height of three miles,
a cobra of smoke,
and Set stood his place,

one foot upon the water
one foot on the dry land,
then did that accursed master of mischief—
Angel of the House of Life—
Osiris,
work his deadly betrayal.

What time Set had stolen his consort, Isis,
who had borne him both Typhon and myself,
Osiris had vowed Set's undoing.
Backed by Anubis,
Osiris wielded a portion of the field
in a manner used for release of the solar energies,
driving suns to the limit of stability.
I had bare warning ere he struck.
Set had none.

Never directed at a planet before,
it destroyed the world.
I escaped,
removing myself to a place light years away.
Typhon tried to flee
to the spaces below where he made his home.
He did not succeed.
I never saw my brother again. Nor thyself, good
        Nephytha.
It cost me a father who was a son,
a brother,
my wife's body;
but it did not destroy the Nameless.

Somehow,
that creature survived the onslaught

of the Hammer that Smashes Suns.
Stunned,
I later found it drifting
amid the world's wreckage,
like a small nebula
hearted with flapping flame.
I worked about it a web of forces,
and, weakened,
it collapsed upon itself.
I removed it then to a secret place
beyond the Worlds of Life,
where it is yet imprisoned
in a room having doors nor windows.
Often have I tried to destroy it,
but I know not what it was that Set discovered
to work its undoing with his Wand.
And still it lives, and yet cries out;

and if ever it is freed,
it could destroy the Life
that is the Middle Worlds.
This is why I never disputed the usurpation
which followed that attack,
and why I still cannot.
I must remain warden,
till Life's adversary is destroyed.

And I could not have prevented what followed:

the Angels of my many Stations,
grown factious in time of my absence,
fell upon one another,
striving for supremacy.

The Wars of the Stations were perhaps thirty years.
Osiris and Anubis reaped what remained at the end.
The other Stations were no more.

Now, of course, these two must rule with great waves
             of the Power,
subjecting the Midworlds to famines,
plagues, wars,
to achieve the balances
much more readily obtained by the gradual,
peaceful actions of the many, of many Stations.
But they cannot do otherwise.
They fear a plurality within the Power.
They would not delegate the Power they had seized.
They cannot co-ordinate it between them.

So, still do I seek a way to destroy the Nameless,
and when this has been done,
shall I turn my energies
to the removal of my Angels
of the two surviving Houses.

This will be easy to accomplish,
though new hands must be ready to work my will.
In the meantime,
it would be disastrous to remove
those who work the greatest good
when two hands stir the tides.

And when this final thing is true,
shall I use the power of these Stations
to re-embody thee, my Nephytha—

Now Nepthytha cries beside the sea and says, "It is too much! It shall never be!" and the Prince Who Was A Thousand stands up and raises his arms.

Within a cloud which hovers before him, there appears the outline of a woman. Perspiration dots his brow, and the woman-form grows more distinct. He steps forward then in an attempt to embarce her, but his arms close only on smoke, and his name, which is the name "Thoth," sounds as a sob within his ears.

Then he is all alone beside the sea, beneath the sea, and the lights in the sky are fishes' bellies digesting fishes' food.

His eyes grow moist before he curses, for he knows it is within her power to end her own existence. He calls her name and there is no reply, not even an echo.

He knows then that the Nameless will die.

He hurls a stone into the ocean and it does not return.

Crossing his arms, he is gone, footprints crumbling in the sand.

Sea birds shriek through the moist air, and a massive reptile rears its green head thirty feet above the waves, long neck swaying, then sinks again beneath the waters a short distance away.

Marachek

Regard now the Citadel of Marachek at Midworlds' Center. . . .

Dead. Dead. Dead. Color it dust.

This is where the Prince Who Was Once A God comes often, to contemplate many things.

There are no oceans on Marachek. There are still a few bubbly springs, these smelling like wet dogs and being warm and brackish. Its sun is a very tired and tiny reddish star, too respectable or too lazy ever to have become a nova and passed out in a burst of glory, shedding a rather anemic light which makes for deep, bluish shadows cast by grotesque stands of stone upon the enormous beach of dun and orange that is Maracheck beneath its winds; and the stars above Marachek may be seen even at midday, faintly, though in the evening they acquire the intensity of neon, acetylene and flash bulb above the windswept plains; and most of Marachek is flat, though the plains rearrange themselves twice daily, when the winds achieve a kind of sterile climax, heaping and unheaping the sands and grinding their grains finer and finer—so that the dust of morning and dusk hangs throughout the day in a yellowish haze, which further detracts from Marachek's eye in the sky—all, ultimately, levelling and settling: the mountains having been ground down, the rocks sculpted and resculpted, and all buried and resurrected perpetually: this is the surface of Marachek, which of course was once a scene of glory, power, pomp and pageantry, its very triteness crying out for this conclusion; but further, there is one building upon Marachek at Midworlds' Center which testifies to the saw's authenticity, this being the Citadel, which doubtless shall exist as long as the world itself, though mayhap the sands shall cover and discover it many times before that day of final dissolution or total frigidity: the Citadel—which is so old that none can say for certain that it was ever built—the Citadel, which may be the oldest city in the universe, broken and repaired (who knows how often?) upon the same foundation, over and over, perhaps since the imaginary beginning of the illusion called Time; the Citadel, which in its very standing testifies that some things *do* endure, no matter how poorly, all vicissitudes—of which Vramin wrote, in *The Proud Fossil:* ". . . The sweetness of decay ne'er touched thy portals, for destiny is amber and sufficient"—the Citadel of Marachek-Karnak, the archetypal city, which is now mainly inhabited by little skittering things, generally insects and reptiles, that feed upon one another, one of which (a toad) exists at this moment of Time beneath an overturned goblet upon an ancient table in Marachek's highest tower (the northeastern) as the sickly sun raises itself from the dust and dusk and the starlight comes down less strongly. This is Marachek.

When Vramin and Madrak enter here, fresh through the gateway from Blis, they deposit their charges upon that ancient table, made all of one piece out of a substance pink and unnatural which Time itself cannot corrupt.

This is the place where the ghosts of Set and the monsters

he fights rage through the marble memory that is wrecked and rebuilt Marachek, the oldest city, forever.

Vramin replaces the General's left arm and right foot; he turns his head so that it faces forward once more, then he makes adjustment upon his neck to hold the head in place.

"How fares the other?" he inquires.

Madrak lowers Wakim's right eyelid and releases his wrist.

"Shock, I'd suppose. Has anyone ever been torn from the center of a fugue battle before?"

"To my knowledge, no. We've doubtless discovered a new syndrome—'fugue fatigue' or 'temporal shock' I'd call it. We may get our names into textbooks yet."

"What do you propose to do with them? Are you able to revive them?"

"Most likely. But then, they'd start in again—and probably keep going till they'd wrecked this world also."

"Not much here to wreck. Perhaps we could sell tickets and turn them loose. Might net a handsome penny."

"Oh, cynical monger of indulgences! 'Twould take a man of the cloth to work a scheme like that!"

"Not so! I learned it on Blis, if you recall."

"True—where life's greatest drawing card had become the fact that it sometimes ends. Nevertheless, in this case, I feel it might be wiser to cast these two upon separate worlds and leave them to their own devices."

"Then why did you bring them here to Marachek?"

"I didn't! They were sucked through the gateway, when I opened it. I aimed for this place myself because the Center is always easiest to reach."

"Then suggestions are now in order as to our immediate course of action."

"Let us rest here awhile, and I will keep these two entranced. We might just open us another gateway and leave them."

"'Twould be against my ethics, brother."

"Speak not to me of ethics, thou inhuman humanist!—Caterer to whatever life-lie man chooses! Th'art an holy ambulance-chaser!"

"Nevertheless, I cannot leave a man to die."

"Very well. . . . Hello! Someone has been here before us, to suffocate a toad!"

Madrak turns his eye upon the goblet.

"I've heard tales that they might endure the ages in tiny, air-less crypts. How long, I wonder, has this one sat thus? If only it lives and could speak! Think of the glories to which it might bear witness."

"Do not forget, Madrak, that I am the poet, and kindly reserve such conjectures to those better able to say them with a straight face. I—"

Vramin moves to the window, and "Company," says he. "Now might we leave these fellows in good conscience."

Upon the battlements, mounted like a statue, Bronze whinnies like a steam whistle and raises three legs and lets them fall. Now he exhales laser beams into the breaking day and his rows of eyes wink on and off.

Something is coming, though still unclear, through the dust and the night.

"Shall we, then?"

"No."

"I share thy sentiment."

Sharing, they wait.

Sexcomp

Now everyone knows that some machines make love, beyond the metaphysical writings of Saint Jakes the Mechanophile, who posits man as the sexual organ of the machine which created him, and whose existence is necessary to fulfill the destiny of mechanism, producing generation after generation of machinekind, all the modes of mechanical evolution flowing through man, until such a time as he has served his purpose, perfection has been reached, and the Great Castration may occur. Saint Jakes is, of course, a heretic. As has been demonstrated on occasions too numerous to cite, the whole machine requires a gender. Now that man and machine undergo frequent interchanges of components and entire systems, it is possible for a complete being to start at any point in the mechman spectrum and to range the entire gamut. Man, the presumptuous organ, has therefore achieved his apotheosis or union with the Gaskethead through sacrifice and redemption, as it were. Ingenuity had much to do with it, but ingenuity of course is a form of mechanical inspiration. One may no longer speak of the Great Castration, no longer consider separating the machine from its creation. Man is here to stay, as a part of the Big Picture.

Everyone knows that machines make love. Not in the crude sense, of course, of those women and men who, for whatever economic purposes may control, lease their bodies for a year or two at a time to one of the vending companies, to be joined with machines, fed intravenously, exercised isometrically, their consciousness submerged (or left turned on, as it would be), to suffer brain implants which stimulate the proper movements for a period not to exceed fifteen minutes per coin, upon the couches of the larger pleasure clubs (and more and more in vogue in the best homes, as well as the cheap street-corner units) for the sport and amusement of their fellows. No. Machines make love via man, but there have been many transferences of function, and they generally do it spiritually.

Consider, however, an unique phenomenon which has just arisen: the Pleasure-Comp—the computer like an oracle, which can answer an enormous range of inquries, and will do so, only for so long as the inquirer can keep it properly stimulated. How many of you have entered the programed boudoir, to have enormous issues raised and settled, and found that time passes so rapidly. Precisely. Reverse-centaur-like—*i.e.*, human from the waist down—it represents the best of two worlds and their fusion into one. There is a love story wrapped up in all this background, as a man enters the Question Room to ask the Dearabbey Machine of his beloved and her ways. It is happening everywhere, always, and there can often be nothing quite so tender. More of this later.

Chief of Missions

Now comes Horus who, seeing Bronze on the wall, deposeth and saith:

"Open this damned gate or I'll kick it down!"

To which Vramin makes reply over the battlement, saying:

"Since I did not fasten it, I am not about to undo it. Find your own entrance or eat dust."

Horus does then kick down the gate, at which Madrak marvels slightly, and Horus then mounts the winding stair to the highest tower. Entering the room, he eyes the poet and the warrior-priest with some malevolence, inquiring:

"Which of you two denied me passage?"

Both step forward.

"A pair of fools! Know you that I am the god Horus, fresh come from the House of Life!"

"Excuse us for not being duly impressed, god Horus," says Madrak, "but none gave us entrance here, save ourselves."

"How be you dead men named?"

"I am Vramin, at your service, more or less."

"... And I, Madrak."

"Ah! I've some knowledge of you two. Why are you here, and what is that carrion on the table?"

"We are here, sir, because we are not elsewhere," says Vramin, "and the table contains two men and a toad—all of whom, I should say, are your betters."

"Trouble can be purchased cheaply, though the refund may be more than you can bear," says Horus.

"What, may I inquire, brings the scantily clad god of vengeance to this scrofulous vicinity?"—Vramin.

"Why, venegance, of course. Has either of you vagabonds set eyes upon the Prince Who Was A Thousand recently?"

"This I must deny, in good faith."

"And I."

"I come seeking him."

"Why here?"

"An oracle, deeming it a propitious spot. And while I am not eager to battle heroes—knowing you as such—I feel you owe me an apology for the entrance I received."

"Fair enough," says Madrak, "for know that our hackles have been raised by a recent battle and we have spent the past hours waxing wroth. Will a swig of good red wine convey our sentiments—coming from what is, doubtless, the only flask of the stuff on this world?"

"It should suffice, if it be of good quality."

"Bide then a moment."

Madrak fetches forth his wine bulb, swigs a mouthful to show it unsullied, casts about the room.

"A fit container, sir," he says, and raises up the down-turned goblet which lies upon the table. Wiping it with a clean cloth, he fills it and proffers it to the god.

"Thank you, warrior-priest. I accept it in the spirit in which it was offered. What battle was it which so upset you that you forgot your manners?"

"That, Brown-eyed Horus, was the battle of Blis, between the Steel General and the one who is called Wakim the Wanderer."

"The Steel General? Impossible! He has been dead for centuries. I slew him myself!"

"Many have slain him. None have vanquished him."

"That pile of junk upon the table? Could that truly be the Prince of Rebels, who one time faced me like a god?"

"Before your memory, Horus, was he mighty," says Vramin, "and when men have forgotten Horus, still will there be a Steel General. It matters not which side he fights upon. Win or lose, he is the spirit of rebellion, which can never die."

"I like not this talk," says Horus. "Surely, if one were to number all his parts and destroy them, one by one, and scatter them across the entire cosmos, then would he cease to exist."

"This thing has been done. And over the centuries have his followers collected him and assembled the engine again. This man, this Wakim, whose like I have never seen before," says Vramin, "voiced a similar sentiment before the fugue battle which racked a world. The only thing which keeps them from laying waste—excuse the poor choice of words—to this world Marachek, is that I will not permit them to awaken again from a state of temporal shock."

"Wakim? This is the deadly Wakim?—Yes. I can believe it as I look upon him in repose. Have you any idea who he is really? Such champions do not spring full-grown from the void."

"I know nothing of him, save that he is a mighty wrestler and a master of the fugue, come to Blis in her last days before the dark tides swept over her—perhaps to hasten their coming."

"That is all you know of him?"

"That is all I know."

"And you, mighty Madrak?"

". . . The sum of my knowledge, also."

"Suppose we were to awaken him and question him?"

Vramin raises his cane.

"Touch him and I shall dispute your passage. He is too fearsome an individual, and we came here to rest."

Horus lays a hand upon Wakim's shoulder and shakes him slightly. Wakim moans.

"Know that the wand of life is also a lance of death!" cries Vramin, and with a lunging motion spears the toad, which sits immediately beside Horus' left hand.

Before Horus can turn upon him, there is a quick outward rush of air as the toad explodes into a towering form in the center of the table.

His long golden hair stands high and his thin lips draw back into a smile, as his green eyes fall upon the tableau at his feet.

The Prince Who Had Been A Toad touches a red spot on his shoulder, says to Vramin, "Did you not know that it has been written, 'Be kind to bird and beast'?"

"Kipling," says Vramin, smiling. "Also, the Koran."

"Shape-shifting miscreant," says Horus, "are you the one I seek—called by many the Prince?"

"I confess to this title. Know that you have disturbed my meditations."

"Prepare to meet your doom," says Horus, drawing an arrow—his only weapon—from his belt, and breaking off its head.

"Do you think that I am unaware of your power, brother?" says the Prince, as Horus raises the arrowhead between thumb and forefinger. "Do you think, brother, that I do not know that you can add the power of your mind to the mass or velocity of any object, increasing it a thousandfold?"

There is a blur in the vicinity of Horus' hand and a crashing sound across the room, as the Prince stands suddenly two feet to the left of where he had been standing and the arrowhead pierces a six-inch wall of metal and continues on into what is now a dusty and windy morning as the Prince continues to speak: ". . . And do you now know, brother, that I could as easily have removed myself an inconceivable distance across space with the same effort that it took me to avoid your shot? Yea, out of the Middle Worlds themselves?"

"Call me not brother," says Horus, raising the shaft of the arrow.

"But thou art my brother," says the Prince. "At least, we'd the same mother."

Horus drops the shaft.

"I believe you not!"

"And from what strain do you think you derived your god-like powers? Osiris? Cosmetic surgery might have given him a chicken's head, and his own dubious strain an aptitude for mathematics—but you and I, shape-shifters both—are sons of Isis, Witch of the Loggia."

"Cursed be my mother's name!"

Suddenly, the Prince stands before him on the floor of the chamber and slaps him with the back of his hand.

"I could have slain you a dozen times over, had I chosen," says the Prince, "as you stood there. But I refrained, for you are my brother. I could slay you now, but I will not. For you are my brother. I bear no arms, for I need none. I bear no malice, or the burden of my life would be staggering. But do not speak ill of our mother, for her ways are her own. I neither praise nor do I blame. I know that you have come here to kill me. If you wish to enjoy an opportunity to do so, you will hold your tongue in this one respect, brother."

"Then let us speak no more of her."

"Very well. You know who my father was, so you know that I am not unversed in the martial arts. I will give you a chance to slay me in hand-to-hand combat, if you will do a thing for me first. Otherwise, I will remove myself and find someone else to assist me, and you may spend the rest of your days seeking me."

"Then this must be what the oracle meant," says Horus, "and it bodes ill for me. Yet I cannot pass up the chance to fulfill my mission, before Anubis' emissary—this Wakim—achieves it. For I know not his powers, which might exceed your own. I will keep my peace, run your errand, and kill you."

"This man is the assassin from the House of the Dead?" says the Prince, looking upon Wakim.

"Yes."

"Were you aware of this, my Angel of the Seventh Station?" asks the Prince.

"No," says Vramin, bowing slightly.

"Nor I, Lord"—Madrak.

"Arouse him—and the General."

"Our bargain is off," says Horus, "if this be done."

"Awaken them both," says the Prince, folding his arms.

Vramin raises his cane, and the green tongues come forth and descend upon the prostrate forms.

Outside, the winds grow more noisy. Horus shifts his attention from one to the other of those present, then speaks: "Your back is to me, brother. Turn around that I may face you as I slay you. As I said, our bargain is off."

The Prince turns.

"I need these men, also."

Horus shakes his head and raises his arm.

Then, "A veritable family reunion," says the voice which fills the chamber, "we three brothers having come together at last."

Horus draws back his hand as from an asp, for the shadow of a dark horse lies between himself and the Prince. He covers his eyes with one hand and lowers his head. "I had forgotten," he says, "that by what I learned today, I am also kin to thee."

"Take it not too badly," says the voice, "for I have known it for ages and learned to live with it."

And Wakim and the Steel General awaken to a sound of laughter that is like the singing wind.

Brotz, Purtz & Dulp

"Pass the frawlpin, please."

"I beg your pardon?"

"The frawlpin! The frawlpin!"

"I don't have it."

"*I've* got it."

"Oh. Why didn't you say so?"

"Why didn't you ask me?"

"Sorry. Just gimme. —Thanks."

"Why do you keep refribbing that job, anyhow? It's ready."

"Just to pass away the time."

"Do you seriously think he'll ever send for it?"

"Of course not. But that's no reason for turning out an inferior product."

"Well, *I* think he'll send for it!"

"Who asked you?"

"I'm volunteering an opinion."

"Whatever would he want it for? A tool no one can use!"

"If he ordered it he wants it. He's the only one of his kind ever comes here to do business, and he's a gentleman, I say. One of these days, he or his'll pop in to pick it up."

"Ha!"

"'Ha!' yourself. Just wait."

"We haven't much choice now."

"Here's your frawlpin back."

"Go sit on it."

Cerberus Yawns

The dog tosses the glove from head to head until, yawning, he misses and it falls to the ground.

He fetches it from among the bones that lie at his feet, wags his tails, curls up and closes four eyes.

His other eyes burn like coals within the massive dark that is behind the Wrong Door.

Above him, in the fallout shelter, the Minotaur bellows. . . .

God Is Love

Fifty thousand devotees of the Old Shoes, led by six castrati-priests, chant a magnificent litany within the stadium.

A thousand drug-maddened warriors, glory glory glory-saying, sway with their spears before the altar of the Unwearable.

It begins to rain, gently, but few notice.

Never to Be

Osiris, holding a skull and depressing a stud on its side, addresses it, saying: "Once mortal, you have come to dwell in the House of Life forever. Once beauty, blooming fair atop a spinal column, you withered. Once truth, you have come to this."

"And who," answers the skull, "is perpetrator of this thing? It is the Lord of the House of Life that will not let me know rest."

And Osiris makes answer, saying: "Know, too, that I use thee for a paperweight."

"If ever thou didst love me, then smash me and let me die! Do not continue to nourish a fragment of her who once loved thee."

"Ah, but dear my lady, one day might I re-embody thee, to feel thy caresses again."

"The thought of this thing repels me."

"And I, also. But one day it might amuse me."

"Dost thou torment all who displease thee?"

"No, no, shell of death, think never that! True, the Angel of the Nineteenth House attempted to slay me, and his nervous

119

system lives, threaded amidst the fibers of this carpet I stand upon; and true, others of my enemies exist in elementary forms at various points within my House—such as fireplaces, ice lockers and ash trays. But think not that I am vindictive. No, never. As Lord of Life, I feel an obligation to repay all things which have threatened life."

"I did not threaten thee, my Lord."

"You threatened my peace of mind."

"Because I resembled thy wife, the Lady Isis?"

"Silence!"

"Aye! I resembled the Queen of Harlots, thy bride. For this reason didst thou desire me and desire my undoing—"

The skull's words are then cut short, however, as Osiris has hurled it against the wall.

As it falls to pieces and chemicals and microminiature circuitry are spread upon the carpet, Osiris curses and falls upon a row of switches at his desk, the depression of which gives rise to a multitude of voices, one of which, above the others, cries out, through the speaker set high upon the wall:

"Oh clever skull, to so have tricked the fink god!"

Consulting the panel and seeing that it is the carpet which has spoken, Osiris moves to the center of the room and begins jumping up and down.

There grows up a field of wailing.

The Power of the Dog

Into the places of darkness and disrepute, upon the world called Waldik, enter the two champions Madrak and Typhon. Sent by Thoth Hermes Trismegistus to steal a glove of singular potency, they are come to do battle with the guardian of that glove. Now, the world Waldik, long ago ravaged, hosts a horde of beings who dwell beneath the surface in caverns and chambers far removed from the courts of day and night. Darkness, dampness, mutation, fratricide, incest and rape are the words most often used by the few who offer commentary upon the world Waldik. Transported there by a piece of spatial hijackery known only to the Prince, the champions will succeed or remain. They go now through burrows, having been told to follow the bellowing.

"Think you, dark horse shadow," asks the warrior-priest, "that thy brother can retrieve us at the proper moment?"

"Yes," replies the shadow that moves at his side. "Though if he cannot, I care not. I can remove myself in my own way whenever I wish."

"Yes, but I cannot."

"Then worry it, fat Dad. I care not. You volunteered to accompany me. I did not request this thing."

"Then into the hands of Whatever May Be that is greater than life or death, I resign myself—if this act will be of any assistance in preserving my life. If it will not, I do not. If my saying this thing at all be presumptuous, and therefore not well received by Whatever may or may not care to listen, then I withdraw the statement and ask forgiveness, if this thing be desired. If not, I do not. On the other hand—"

"Amen! And silence, please!" rumbles Typhon. "I have heard a thing like a bellow—to our left."

Sliding invisibly along the dark wall, Typhon rounds the bend and moves ahead. Madrak squints through infrared glasses and splays his beam like a blessing upon everything encountered.

"These caverns be deep and vasty," he whispers.

There is no reply.

Suddenly he comes to a door which may be the right door.

Opening it, he meets the minotaur.

He raises his staff, but the thing vanishes in a twinkling.

"Where . . . ?" he inquires.

"Hiding," says Typhon, suddenly near, "somewhere within the many twistings and turnings of its lair."

"Why is this?"

"It would seem that its kind are hunted by creatures much like yourself, both for food and man/bull-headed trophies. It fears direct battle, therefore, and retreats—for man uses weapons upon cattle. Let us enter the labyrinth and hope not to see it again. The entranceway we seek, to the lower chambers, lies somewhere within."

For perhaps half a day they wander, unsuccessfully seeking the Wrong Door. Three doors do they come upon, but only bones lie behind.

"I wonder how the others fare?" asks the warrior-priest.

"Better, or worse—or perhaps the same," replies the other, and laughs.

Madrak does not laugh.

Coming into a circle of bones, Madrak sees the charging beast barely in time. He raises his staff and begins the battle.

He strikes it between the horns and upon the side. He jabs, slashes at, pushes, strikes the creature. He locks with it and wrestles, hand to hand.

Hurting one another, they strive, until finally Madrak is raised from the floor and hurled across the chamber, to land upon his left shoulder on a pile of bones. As he struggles to raise himself, he is submerged by an ear-breaking bellow. Head lowered, the minotaur charges. Madrak finds his feet and begins to rise.

But a dark horse shadow falls upon the creature, and it is gone—completely and forever.

He bows his head and chants the Possibly Proper Death Litany.

"Lovely," snorts his companion, when he comes to the final "Amen." "Now, fat Dad, I think I have found us the Wrong Door. I might enter without opening it, but you may not. How would you have it?"

"Bide a moment," says Madrak, standing. "A bit of narcotic and I'll be good as new and stronger than before. Then we shall enter together."

"Very well. I'll wait."

Madrak injects himself and after a time is like unto a god.

"Now show me the door and let us go in."

"This way."

And there is the door, big and forbidding and colorless, within the infra-light.

"Open it," says Typhon, and Madrak does.

In the firelight it plays, worrying the gauntlet. Perhaps the size of two and a half elephants, it sports with its toy there atop a heap of bones. One of its heads sniffs at the sudden draft of air from beyond the Wrong Door, two of its heads snarl and the third drops the glove.

"Do you understand my voice?" asks Typhon, but there is no answering intelligence behind its six red eyes. Its tails twitch and it stands, all scaley and impervious, within the flicker and glow.

"Nice doggie," comments Madrak, and it wags its tails, opens its mouths and lunges toward him.

"Kill it!" cries Madrak.

"That is impossible," answers Typhon. "In time, that is."

A Pair of Soles
Upon the Altar

Coming at length to the world Interludici, and entering through the sudden green gateway the poet hurls upon the blackness, Wakim and Vramin enter the mad world of many rains and religions. Lightfooted, they stand upon the moist turf outside a city of terrible black walls.

"We shall enter now," says the poet, stroking his sky-green beard. "We shall enter through that small door off to the left, which I shall cause to open before us. Then will we hypnotize or subdue any guards who may be present and make our way into the heart of the city, where the great temple stands."

"To steal boots for the Prince," says Wakim. "This is a strange employment for one such as myself. Were it not for the fact that he had promised to give my name back to me—my real name—before I slay him, I would not have agreed to do this thing for him."

"I realize that, Lord Randall, my son," says Vramin, "but tell me, what do you intend to do with Horus, who would also slay him—and who works for him now only to gain this same opportunity?"

"Slay Horus first, if need be."

"The psychology behind this thing fascinates me, so I trust you will permit me one more question: What difference does it make whether you slay him or Horus slays him? He will be just as dead either way."

Wakim pauses, apparently considering the matter, as if for the first time.

"This thing is *my* mission, not his," he says at length.

"He will be just as dead, either way," Vramin repeats.

"But not by my hand."

"True. But I fail to see the distinction."

"So do I, for that matter. But it is *I* who have been charged with the task."

"Perhaps Horus has also."

"But not by *my* master."

"Why should you have a master, Wakim? Why are you not your own man?"

Wakim rubs his forehead.

"I—do not—really—know. . . . But I must do as I am told."

"I understand," says Vramin, and, while Wakim is thus distracted, a tiny green spark arcs between the tip of the poet's cane and the back of Wakim's neck.

He slaps at his neck then and scratches it.

"What . . . ?"

"A local insect," says the poet. "Let us proceed to the door."

The door opens before them, beneath the tapping of his cane, and its guards drowse before a brief green flare. Appropriating cloaks from two of them. Wakim and Vramin move on, into the center of the city.

The temple is easy enough to find. Entering it is another matter.

Here now, there are guards—drug-maddened—before the entrance.

They approach boldly and demand admission.

The eighty-eight spears of the Outer Guard are leveled at them.

"There will be no public adoration till the sundown rains," they are told, amidst twitches.

"We shall wait." And they do.

With the sundown rains, they join a procession of moist worshippers and enter the outer temple.

On attempting to go further they are brought to a halt by the three hundred fifty-two drug-maddened spearmen who guard the next entranceway.

"Have you the badges of inner-temple worshippers?" their captain inquires.

"Of course," says Vramin, raising his cane.

And in the eyes of the captain they must have them, for they are granted entrance.

Then, drawing near the Inner Sanctum itself, they are halted by the officer in charge of the five hundred ten drug-maddened warriors who guard the way.

"Castrated or non-castrated?" he inquires.

"Castrated, of course," says Vramin in a lovely soprano. "Give us entrance," and his eyes blaze greenly and the officer draws back.

Entering, they spy the altar, with its fifty guardians and its six strange priests.

"There they are, upon the altar."

"How shall we obtain them?"

"By stealth, preferably," says Vramin, pushing his way nearer the altar, before the televised service begins.

"What sort of stealth?"

"Perhaps we can substitute a pair of our own and wear the sacred ones out of here."

"I'm game."

"Then, suppose they were stolen five minutes ago?"

"I understand you," says Wakim and bows his head, as in adoration.

The service begins.

"Hail to Thee, Shoes," lisps the first priest, "wearer of feet . . ."

"Hail!" chant the other five.

"Good, kind, noble and blessed Shoes."

"Hail!"

". . . which came to us from chaos . . ."

"Hail!"

". . . to lighten our hearts and uplift our soles."

"Hail!"

"Oh Shoes, which have supported mankind since the dawn of civilization . . ."

"Hail!"

"ultimate cavities, surrounders of feet."

"Hail!"

"Hail! Wondrous, battered Buskins!"

"We adore thee."

"We adore thee!"

"We worship thee in the fulness of thy Shoeness!"

"Glory!"

"Oh archetypal footgear!"

"Glory!"

"Supreme notion of Shoes."

"Glory!"

"What could we do without thee?"

"What?"

"Stub our toes, scratch our heels, have our arches go flat."

"Hail!"

"Protect us, thy worshipers, good and blessed Footgear!"

"Which came to us from chaos . . ."

". . . on a day dark and drear . . ."

". . . out of the void, burning—"

". . . but not burnt . . ."

". . . Thou hast come to comfort and support us . . ."

"Hail!"

". . . upright, forthright and forward forever!"

"Forever!"

Wakim vanishes.

A cold, wild wind begins.

It is the change-wind out of time; and there is a blurring upon the altar.

Seven previously drug-maddened spearmen lie sprawled, their necks at unusual angles.

Suddenly, beside Vramin, Wakim says, "Pray, find us a gateway quickly!"

"You wear them?"

"I wear them."

Vramin raises his cane, pauses.

"There will be a brief delay, I fear," and his gaze grows emerald.

All eyes in the temple are suddenly upon them.

Forty-three drug-maddened spearmen shout a battle cry as one, and leap forward.

Wakim crouches and extends his hands.

"Such is the kingdom of heaven," comments Vramin, perspiration like absinthe glittering coldly upon his brow. "I wonder how the video tapes will show this thing."

129

Weft and Wand

"What is this place?" Horus cries out.

The Steel General stands braced, as for an anticipated shock, but there is none.

"We are come to a place that is not a world, but simply a place," says the Prince Who Was A Thousand. "There is no ground to stand upon, nor need of it here. There is little light, but those who dwell in this place are blind, so it does not matter. The temperature will suit itself to any living body, because those who dwell here wish it so. Nourishment is drawn from this air like water, through which we move, so there is no need to eat. And such is the nature of this place that one need never sleep here."

"It sounds rather like Hell," Horus observes.

"Nonsense," says the Steel General. "My own existence is just so, as I carry my environment around with me. I am not discomfited."

"Hell," Horus repeats.

"At any rate, take my hands," says the Prince, "and I will guide

130

you across the darkness and amid the glowing motes of light until we reach the ones I seek."

They link hands, the Prince furls his cloak, and they drift through the twilitic landscape that is empty of horizon.

"And *where* is this place that is not a world?" asks the General.

"I do not know," says the Prince. "Perhaps it only exists in some deep and shiny corner of my dark and dirty mind. All that I really know is the way to reach it."

Falling, drifting a timeless time, they come at last to a tent like a gray cocoon, flickering, above/below/before them.

The Prince disengages his hands and places his fingertips upon its surface. It quivers then, and an opening appears, through which he passes, a "follow me" drifting back over his shoulder.

Brotz, Purtz and Dulp sit within, doing something which would be quite disgusting and unique by human standards, but which is normal and proper for them, since they are not human and have different standards.

"Greetings, smiths of Norn," says the Prince. "I have come to obtain that which I ordered a time ago."

"I told you he'd come!" cries one of the grayish mounds, twitching its long, moist ears.

"I acknowledge that you were correct," answers another.

"Yes. Where's that frawlpin? I ought to refrib it once more, before . . ."

"Nonsense! It's perfect."

"It *is* ready then?" inquires the Prince.

"Oh, it's been ready for ages. Here!"

The speaker draws a length of cold blue light from a sheath of black fabric and offers it to the Prince. The Prince takes it into his hand, inspects it, nods and replaces it within the sheath.

"Very good."

". . . And the payment?"

"I have them here." The Prince withdraws a dark case from beneath his cloak and places it in the air before him, where of course it hangs suspended. "Which of you will be first?"

"He will."

"She will."

"It will."

"Since you cannot decide, I will have to do the choosing myself."

The Prince opens the case, whcih contains surgical apparatus and an extrusible operating light, as all three creatures begin to quiver in their places.

"What is happening?" inquires Horus, who has entered now and stands beside him.

"I am about to operate on these fellows, and I will require your enormous strength in assistance, as well as the General's."

"Operate? To what end?" asks the General.

"They have no eyes," says the Prince, "and they would see again. I've brought three pairs with me and I'm going to install them."

"This would require extensive neurological adaptation."

"This has already been done."

"By whom?"

"Myself, the last time I gave them eyes."

"What became of those?"

"Oh, they seldom last. After a time, their bodies reject them. Generally, though, their neighbors blind them."

"Why is that?"

"I believe it is because they go about boasting how, among all their people, only they are able to see. This results in a speedy democratization of affairs."

"Ghastly!" says the General, who has lost count of his own blindings. "I'm minded to stay and fight for them."

"They would refuse your assistance," says the Prince. "—Would you not?"

"Of course," says one of them.

"We would not employ a mercenary against our own people," says another.

"It would violate their rights," says the third.

"What rights?"

"Why, to blind us, of course. What sort of barbarian are you?"

"I withdraw my offer."

"Thank you."

"Thank you."

"Thank you."

"What assistance will you require?" asks Horus.

"The two of you must seize upon my patient and hold him, while I perform the surgery."

"Why is that?"

"Because they are incapable of unconsciousness and no local anesthetics will affect them."

"You mean you are going to perform delicate surgery on them just as they are—exotic surgery, at that?"

"Yes. That is why I will need two of you to immobilze each patient. They are quite strong."

"Why must you do this thing?"

"Because they want it done. It is the price agreed upon for their labors."

"Whatever for? A few weeks' seeing? And then—what is there to see in this place, anyhow? It is mainly dust, darkness, a few feeble lights."

"It is their wish to look upon each other—and their tools. They are the greatest artisans in the universe."

"Yes, I want to see a frawlpin again—if Dulp hasn't lost it."

"And I, a gult."

"I, a crabwick."

"That which they desire costs them pain, but it will give them memories to last for ages."

"Yes, it is worth it," says one, "so long as I am not the first."

"Nor I."

"Nor I."

The Prince lays out his instruments in the middle of the air, sterilizes them and points a finger.

"That one," he says, and the screaming begins.

The General turns off his hearing and much of his humanity for the next several hours. Horus is reminded of his father's study; also of Liglamenti, on D'donori. The Prince's hands are steady.

When it is done, the creatures have bandages over their faces, which they may not remove for a time. All three are moaning and crying out. The Prince cleans his hands.

"Thank you, Prince Who Was A Surgeon," says one of the creatures.

". . . for this thing you have done for us."

". . . and for us."

"You are welcome, goodly Norns. Thank you for a wand well made."

"Oh, it was nothing."

". . . Let us know whenever you need another."

". . . And the price will be the same."

"Then I shall be going now."

"Good-bye."

"Farewell."

"Adieu."

"Good seeing to you, my fellows."

And the Prince takes Horus and the General in hand, setting all feet upon the road to Marachek, which is but one step away.

Behind him there is more wailing, and things quite normal and proper for Norns are quickly and frantically done.

They are back in the Citadel almost before Horus, who knows what it is, has succeeded in drawing the blue wand from its sheath at the Prince's side.

It is a duplicate of the weapon which sun-eyed Set had used against the Nameless, a thousand years before.

The Temptation of
Saint Madrak

Madrak has one chance of living through the onslaught. He throws his staff and dives forward.

The choice is the right one.

He passes beneath the dog as it leaps, snapping at his staff.

His hand falls upon the strange fabric of the glove the creature had been worrying.

Suddenly, he is comforted by a confidence in his invincibility. This is something even the narcotic had not fully instilled in him.

Quickly he determines the cause and slips the glove upon his right hand.

The dog turns as Typhon rears.

The black shadow falls between them.

Tickling, stirring, the glove reaches to Madrak's elbow, spreads across his back, his chest.

The dog lunges and then howls, for the dark horse shadow comes upon it. One head hangs lifeless as the others snarl.

"Depart, oh Madrak, to the appointed place!" says Typhon.

"I shall occupy this creature to its destruction and follow in my own way!"

The glove moves down his left arm, covers the hand, spreads across his chest, reaches down to his waist.

Madrak, who has always been mighty, suddenly reaches forth and crushes a stone within his right hand.

"I fear it not, Typhon. I'll destroy it myself."

"In my brother's name, I bid thee go!"

Bowing his head, Madrak departs. Behind him, the sounds of battle rage. He moves through the lair of the minotaur. He makes his way upward through the corridors.

Pale creatures with green, glowing eyes accost him. He slays them easily with his hands and proceeds.

When the next group of attackers moves upon him, he subdues them but does not slay them, having had time to think.

Instead he says:

"It might be good for you to consider the possibility of your having portions of yourselves which might withstand the destruction of your bodies, and to label these hypothetical quantities souls, for the sake of argument. Now then, beginning with the proposition that such—"

But they attack him again and he is forced to slay them all.

"Pity," he says, and repeats the Possibly Proper Death Litany.

Proceeding upward, he comes at last to the appointed place.

And there he stands.

At the Gateway to the Underworld . . .

On Waldik . . .

"Hell hath been harrowed," he says. "I am half invincible. This must be the gauntlet of Set. Strange that it but half covers me. But perhaps I'm more a man than he was." *Stomach then regarded.* "And perhaps not. But the power that lies in this thing . . . Mighty! To beat the filthy-souled into submission and effect their conversions—perhaps this is why it was rendered unto my hand. Is Thoth divine? Truly, I do not know. I wonder. If he is, then I wrong him by not delivering it. —Unless, of course, this be his secret will." *Regards hands enmeshed.* "My power is now beyond measure. How shall I use it? All of Waldik might I convert with this instrument, given but time." Then, "But he charged me with a specific task. —Yet . . ." *Smile. (The mesh does not cover his face.)* "What if he is divine? Sons who beget their fathers may well be. I recall the myth of Eden. I know this serpent-like glove may indicate the Forbidden." *Shrugs.* "But the good which might be done . . . No! It is a trap! But I could beat the Words into their heads. . . . I'll do it! 'Though Hell gape wide,' as Vramin says."

But as he turns he is caught up in a vortex that sucks the words from his throat and casts him down a wide, blank, cold well.

Behind him, the shadows strive, Waldik gapes wide, and then he is gone, for the Prince has called him home.

Thundershoon

. . . **B**ut Wakim the Wanderer has donned the shoes, and he rises now to stand in the middle of the air, laughing. With each step that he takes, a sonic boom goes forth from the temple to mingle with the thunder. The warriors and the worshipers bow down.

Wakim runs up the wall and stands upon the ceiling.

A green door appears at Vramin's back.

Wakim descends and steps through it.

Vramin follows.

"Hail!" suggests one of the priests.

But the drug-maddened spearmen turn upon him and rend him.

One day, long after their miraculous departure, a galaxy of mighty warriors will set forth upon the Quest of the Holy Shoes.

In the meantime, the altar is empty, the evening rains come down.

Winning the Wand

On Marachek, in the Citadel, stand they all, there, as backward reel their minds.

"I've the shoes," says Wakim. "You may have them for my name."

"I've the glove," says Madrak and turns away his face.

". . . And I've the wand," says Horus, and it falls from his hand.

"It did not pass through me," says the Prince, "because it is not formed of matter, nor any other thing over which you may exercise control." And the mind of the Prince is closed to the inner eye of Horus.

Horus steps forward, and his left leg is longer than his right leg, but he is perfectly balanced upon the now uneven floor; the window burns like a sun at the Prince's back, and the Steel General is turned to gold and flowing; Vramin burns like a taper and Madrak becomes a fat doll bounding at the end of a rubber strand; the walls growl and pulse in and out with a regular rhythm keeping time with the music that comes from the shuffling bars of the spectrum upon the floor at the end of the tunnel that begins with the window and lies like burning honey and the tiger above the wand now grown monstrous and too fine to behold within the eternity of the tower room in the Citadel of Marachek at Midworlds' Center where the Prince has raised his smile.

Horus advances another step, and his body is transparent to his sense, so that all things within him become immediately known and frightening.

"Oh the moon comes like a genie
    from the Negro lamp of night,
        and the tunnel of my seeing is her roadway.
    She raises up the carpet of the days
        I've walked upon,
            and through caverns of the sky we make our
                pathway,"

says a voice strangely like yet unlike Vramin's.

And Horus raises his hand against the Prince.

But the Prince already holds his wrist in a grip that burns.

And Horus raises up his other hand against the Prince.

But the Prince already holds that wrist in a grip that freezes.

And he raises up his other hand and electrical shocks pass along it.

And he raises up his other hand and it blackens and dies.

And he raises up a hundred hands more and they turn to snakes and fight among themselves and of course he whispers: "What has happened?"

"A world," says the Prince, "to which I have transported us."

"It is unfair to choose such a battleground," says Horus, "a world too like the one I know—only a fraction away and so twisted," and his words are all the colors of Blis and round and dripping.

"And it is indecent of you to want to kill me."

"I have been charged with this thing, and it is my will also."

"So you have failed," says the Prince, forcing him to kneel upon the Milky Way, which becomes a transparent intestinal tract, racked by a rapid peristalsis.

The smell is overpowering.

"No!" whispers Horus.

"Yes, brother. You are defeated. You cannot destroy me. I have bested you. It is time to quit, to resign, to go home."

"Not until I have accomplished my objective."

The stars, like ulcers, burn within his guts, and Horus pits the strength of his body against the kaleidoscope that is the Prince. The Prince drops to one knee, but with his genuflection there comes a hail of hosannas from the innumerable dog-faced flowers that bloom upon his brow like sweat and merge to a mask of glass which cracks and unleashes lightnings. Horus pushes his arms toward the nineteen moons which are being eaten by the serpents his fingers; and who calls out, oh God, but conscience his father, birdheaded on sky's throne and weeping blood? Resign? Never! Go home? The red laughter comes as he strikes at the brother-faced thing below.

"Yield and die!"

Then cast . . .

. . . far forth

. . . where Time is dust

and days are lilies without number . . .

and the night is a purple cockatrice whose name is oblivion denied . . .

He becomes a topless tree chopped through and falling forever.

At the end of forever, he lies upon his back and stares up at the Prince Who is his Brother, standing at all heights with eyes that imprison him.

"I give you leave to depart now, brother, for I have beaten you fairly," come the green words.

Then Horus bows his head and the world departs and the old world comes again.

"Brother, I wish you had slain me," he says, and coughs behind his bruises.

"I cannot."

"Do not send me back with this kind of defeat upon me."

"What else am I to do?"

"Grant me some measure of mercy. I know not what."

"Then hear me and go with honor. Know that I would slay your father, but that I will spare him for your sake if he will but aid me when the time arises."

"What time?"

"That is for him to decide."

"I do not understand."

"Of course not. But bear him the message, anyway."

" . . . "

"Agreed?"

"Agreed," says Horus and begins to rise.

When he regains his feet, he realizes that he is standing in the Hall of the Hundred Tapestries, and alone. But in that last, agonizing instant, he learned a thing.

He hastens to write it down.

People, Places and Things

"Where is Horus?" inquires Madrak. "He was here but a moment ago."

"He has gone home," says the Prince, rubbing his shoulder. "Now let me name you my problem—"

"My name," says Wakim, "give it to me. Now."

"Yes," says the Prince, "I will give it to you. You are a part of the problem I was about to name."

"Now," Wakim repeats.

"Do you feel any different with those shoes upon your feet?"

"Yes."

"How so?"

"I don't know. . . . Give me my name."

"Give him the glove, Madrak."

"I don't want a glove."

"Put it on, if you wish to know you name."

"Very well."

He dons the glove.

"Now do you know your name?"

"No. I . . ."

"What?"

"It feels familiar, very familiar, to have the mesh spread across my body . . ."

"Of course."

"It can't be!" says Madrak.

"No?" the Prince inquires. "Pick up that wand and hold it, Wakim. —Here, hang its sheath about your waist . . ."

"What are you doing to me?"

"Restoring what is rightfully yours."

"By what right?"

"Pick up the wand."

"I don't want to! You can't make me! You promised me my name. Say it!"

"Not until you've picked up the wand."

The Prince takes a step toward Wakim. Wakim backs away. "No!"

"Pick it up!"

The Prince advances further. Wakim retreats.

"I—may not!"

"You may."

"Something about it . . . It is forbidden that I touch that instrument."

"Pick it up and you will learn your name—your true name."

"I— No! I don't want my name any more! Keep my name!"

"You *must* pick it up."

"No!"

"It is written that you must pick it up."

"Where? How?"

"I have written it, I—"

"Anubis!" cries Wakim. "Hear my prayer! I call upon thee in all thy power! Attend me in this place where I stand in the midst of thy enemies! The one whom I must destroy is at hand! Aid me against him, as I offer him to thee!"

Vramin encircles himself, Madrak and the General with elaborate spikes of green flame.

The wall at Wakim's back slowly dissolves, and infinity is there.

Arm hanging limp, dog-faced jeering, Anubis stares down.

"Excellent, servant!" come the words. "You have found him, cornered him. But the final blow remains, and your mission is done. Use the fugue!"

"No," says the Prince, "he will not destroy me, even with the fugue, while I have this thing for him: You recognized him when first you saw him, long ago. His true name is now near to his ears. He would hear it spoken."

"Do not listen to him, Wakim," says Anubis. "Kill him now!"

"Master, is it true that he knows my name? My real name?"

"He lies! Slay him!"

"I do not lie. —Pick up the wand and you will know the truth."

"Do not touch it! It is a trap! You will die!"

"Would I go through all these elaborate motions to slay you in this manner, Wakim? Whichever of us dies at the hands of the other, the dog will win. He knows it, and he sent you to do a monstrous act. See how he laughs!"

"Because I have won, Thoth! He comes to kill you now!"

Wakim advances upon the Prince, then stoops and picks up the wand.

He screams, and even Anubis draws back.

Then the sound of his throat turns to laughter.

He raises the wand.

"Silence, dog! You have used me! Oh, how you have used me! You apprenticed me to death for a thousand years, that I might slay my son and my father without flinching. But now you look upon Set the Destroyer, and your days are numbered!" His eyes glow through the mesh which covers his entire body, and he stands above the floor. A line of blue light lances from

146

the wand that he holds, but Anubis is gone, faded with a quick gesture and an half-heard howl.

"My son," says Set, touching Thoth's shoulder.

"My son," says the Prince, bowing his head.

The spikes of green flame fall behind them.

Somewhere, a dark thing cries out within the light, within the night.

Words

Between you and me,
the words,
like mortar,
separating, holding together
those pieces of the structure ourselves.

To say them,
to cast their shadows on the page,
is the act of binding mutual passions,
is cognizance, yourself/myself,
of our sameness under skin;
it rears possible cathedrals
indicating infinity with steeply-high styli.

For when tomorrow comes it is today,
and if it is not the drop
that is eternity
glistening at the pen's point,

then the ink of our voices
surrounds like an always night,
and mortar marks the limit of our cells.

"What does it mean?" asks Lord Uiskeagh the Red, who is out with twenty men to raise the Border-side against Dilwit of Liglamenti.

His party leans through fog toward the rock where the words are graven.

"Lord, I've heard of these things," remarks his captain. "They are the doings of the poet Vramin, who publishes in this manner: He casts his poems at the nearest world, and wherever they fall they record themselves upon the hardiest substance handy. He boasts that he has written parables, sermons and poems in stones, leaves and brooks."

"Oh, he does, does he? Well, what's this one mean? Is it to be taken as a good omen?"

"It means nothing, Lord, for it's common knowledge that he's also mad as a golind at rutting time."

"Well, then, let us urinate upon it and be on our way to the wars."

"Very good, Lord."

Shadow and Substance

"Father?" says the dark horse shadow upon the castle wall.

"Yes, Typhon."

"Father!"

A sound to break the ears occurs, then:

"Anubis said you had perished!"

"He lied. Osiris must have wielded the Hammer, saying that he was saving the universe, for I was losing the battle."

"That is true," says the Prince.

"I was not losing, however; I was winning. He wished to slay me, not the Nameless."

"How did you survive?"

"A reflex. I went into fugue as the blow descended. A fraction of it fell upon me and Anubis retrieved me, senseless, and spirited me off to his House. He scattered my gear across the Midworlds. He trained me as his weapon."

"To slay Thoth?"

"That was the task he gave me."

"Then he dies!" says Typhon and rears, flaming.

"Desist, brother," says the Prince. "He did not succeed, and we may yet have a use for the dog. . . ."

But already the dark horse shadow has faded, and the Prince lowers his head.

He looks to Set.

"Should we follow to stop him?"

"Why? Anubis has lived a thousand years too long. Let him guard himself now. —And how? Even if we would, there is none can stop Typhon when the madness lies upon him."

"That is true," says the Prince, and, turning, he addresses Vramin:

"If you would serve me further, my former Angel of the Seventh Station, go you to the House of the Dead. It will soon require the presence of one who can operate the machinery."

"Typhon was Lord of the House of Fire," says Vramin.

"Yes, but I fear he will not remain in the House of the Dead after he has gained vengeance. If I know my brother, he will then seek out the one who wielded the Hammer. He will go after Osiris."

"Then I shall remove me to the House of the Dead. Will you accompany me, Madrak?"

"If the Prince has no further use for me here."

"I have not. You may go."

"Lord," says Vramin, "it is kind of you to trust me again, knowing the part I played in the Wars of the Stations. . . ."

"Those days are gone, and we are different people—are we not?"

"I hope so—and thank you."

The Prince crosses his arms and bows his head. Vramin and Madrak vanish.

"How," says the Steel General, "may I assist you?"

"We go again to fight the Nameless," says the Prince Who Was A Thousand. "Will you come and stand in reserve?"

"Yes. Let me summon Bronze."

"Do so."

The winds of Marachek stir the dust. The sun flickers its way into another day.

Master of
the House of the Dead

Vramin stands in the great Hall of the House of the Dead, holding his Maypole cane. Its streamers go forth, entering into all the passageways, visible or otherwise, which come together at that place.

At his side, Madrak shifts his weight from foot to foot and stares about him.

Vramin's eyes glow, and the light dances within them.

"Nothing. Nothing alive. Nowhere," he says.

"Then Typhon has found him," says Madrak.

"Then Typhon is not here either."

"Then he has slain him and departed. He doubtless seeks Osiris now."

"I wonder. . . ."

"What else could it be?"

"I do not know. But now I am master here, by delegation of the Prince. I will find the places of power and learn their functions."

"Yet once you broke faith with the Prince. . . ."

"That is true—and he forgave me."

Then Vramin seats himself upon the throne of Anubis, and Madrak pays him homage, saying:

"Hail, Vramin! Master of the House of the Dead!"

"You need bend no knee to me, old friend. Please rise. I will need your assistance, for this place is quite different from the Seventh Station, where once I reigned."

And for hours Vramin studies the secret controls about the throne. Then, "Anubis!" cries a voice which he knows is not the voice of Madrak.

And somehow he mimics the bark, the whine:

"Yes?"

"You were right. Horus was defeated, and he returned here. But he is gone again."

It is the voice of Osiris.

He gestures with his cane, and the big window appears in the middle of the air.

"Hello, Osiris," he says.

"So the Prince has finally moved," says Osiris. "I suppose I am next."

"I hope not," says Vramin. "I can personally attest to having heard the Prince assure Horus that he would not take vengeance upon you—in exchange for cooperation."

"Then what has become of Anubis?"

"I do not know for certain. Typhon came here to kill him. I came here to clean up after Typhon and to hold the Station. Either he has slain him and departed, or Anubis fled and Typhon followed. So listen to me, Osiris: Despite the Prince's assurance, you are in danger. Typhon is not aware of the Prince's promise, and he was not party to it. Having learned the true story from Set himself and having heard it confirmed by the Prince, he is likely to seek vengeance on the wielder of the Hammer—"

"Set lives?"

"Yes. He was known for a time as Wakim."

"Anubis' emissary!"

"None other. The dog had stripped him of his memories and sent him to slay his own son—and father. That is what moved Typhon to anger."

"A pox on the whole bloody family! And what has become of my son? He but left me this note, and—Of course!"

"'Of course,' what?"

"It is not too late. I—"

"Behind you, on the wall!" cries Vramin. "Typhon!"

Osiris moves with a speed which belies his fragile appearance. He dives toward a green tapestry, casts it aside and moves beyond.

The shadow flows after him and rears.

When it moves away, there is a Typhon-shaped hole in the tapestry and the wall itself.

"Typhon," says Vramin.

"I am here," comes the voice. "Why did you give warning?"

"Because Thoth gave him his life."

"I was not aware of this."

"You did not remain long enough to hear it repeated. Now it is too late."

"No. I fear he has escaped me."

"How so?"

"He was not within the chamber when I destroyed it."

"This may be a good thing. Listen. We can use Osiris."

"No! There can never be peace between our families so long as he lives, regardless of any chivalrous sentiments my brother may mouth. I love my brother, but I will not abide by his forgiving this one. No. I will search this House until I find Osiris and he passes down Skagganauk Abyss!"

"As did Anubis?"

"No! Anubis has escaped me!" comes the cry. "For a time."

155

Then Typhon rears, the flames come, and he is gone.

Vramin makes a daisy-beheading gesture with his cane, and the window is closed.

"Anubis still lives," says Madrak, looking back over his shoulder.

"Obviously."

"What shall we do?"

"We shall continue to study the functions of the House of the Dead."

"I wish to rest."

"Then do so. Find yourself a near chamber and retire. You know where the food is."

"Yes."

"Till later, then."

"Till later, Lord."

Madrak goes forth from the great Hall, and he wanders. He comes, after a time, to a chamber where the dead stand like statues. He seats himself among them. He speaks.

"I was his faithful servant. Hear me, lady with the breasts like melons. —I was his faithful servant. The poet went to war with other Angels, knowing it went against his will. But he is forgiven and exalted. And where am I? Servant to a servant."

It is not fair.

"I'm glad you agree with me. —And you there, fellow with the extra arms. Did you spread religion and morality? Did you single-handedly defeat monsters and wondrous beasts among the unenlightened?"

Of course not.

"So you see . . ." He slaps his thigh. "So you see, there is no justice, and virtue is constantly betrayed, befouled, imposed upon. Look what has become of the General, who devoted his life to humanity: Life took away his own humanity. Is *that* justice?"

Hardly.

"All comes to this, my brothers. We all become statues in the House of the Dead, regardless of the lives we led. The universe never thanks. The giver is never repaid. —Oh, You Who May Be, why did You make things to be this way—if You did make things to be this way, that is—why? I have tried to serve You and the Prince Your Agent. What has it gotten me? Coach fare and third-class accommodations. I am glad that Set battles the Nameless without the gauntlet of power—"

"What?"

And looking up, he sees a statue which had not been there before; and unlike the others, it moves.

Its head is the head of a black dog, and its red tongue darts and curls.

"You! How could you have hidden from Vramin, escaped Typhon?"

"This is my House. It will be many ages before all its secrets may be learned by another."

Madrak stands, and his staff spins in his hands.

"I do not fear you, Anubis. I have fought in every clime and place where man may take the Word. I have sent many to this House, and I come myself as a conqueror, not as a victim."

"You were conquered long ago, Madrak, and you only just now realized it."

"Silence, dog! You speak to one who holds your life in his hands."

"And you speak to one who holds your future in his."

"What do you mean?"

"You said that Set goes to battle the Nameless once again?"

"That is true. And when the Nameless has been destroyed, the millennium will come."

"Ha! Save your metaphysics, preacher. Answer me another thing, and I will tell you a very good thing indeed."

"What thing?"

Anubis steps forward, limp arm fluttering at his side.

"What of the gauntlet of power?"

"Oh," says Madrak, removing a gauntlet from beneath his dark garment and drawing it upon his right hand. "When I obtained this item, I thought that worlds might be won for the faith with it." It reaches to his elbow, his shoulder. "I did not know that Wakim was Set. I was tempted to keep it for myself. So I substituted my own gauntlet-that-grows. It is a common enough item in some places among the Midworlds. This one seems to be of peculiar potency, while the other is but ordinary armor." The gauntlet now flares to cover his back, his chest.

"I could kiss thy fat cheeks!" says Anubis. "For Set will now have less of a chance against the Nameless. —And all along you planned this betrayal! You are a shrewder man than I'd supposed, Dad!"

"I was used and I was tempted. . . ."

"But no more shalt thou be used. Oh no! Now you wear the glove, and I propose an alliance—"

"Back dog! You're not better than anyone else! I've something you want now and my backside is suddenly kissing-sweet. Oh no! Whatever I do with my newfound power, I do for one person: Me!"

"The alliance I propose will be mutually beneficial."

"I need but give the alarm and you will be bound so tightly that all your guile will not serve to free you. I need but spin my staff in the proper manner and your brains will decorate the walls. So speak now, with that in mind, fork-tongue, and I will listen."

"If Osiris still lives," says Anubis, "and if we can reach him, then we three together may be able to destroy Thoth."

"I am sure that Osiris still lives—though for how much longer this will be so, I cannot say. Typhon pursues him about the House of Life at this moment."

"We've a chance, a very good chance, of recovering all—

now that you hold the gauntlet. I've got a way to get to the House of Life, and perhaps a way to rescue Osiris, also."

"Then what? We do not even know where the battle with the Nameless is occurring."

"One thing by itself, another when it arises. Are you with me?"

"I'll go along with you to the House of Life, as Thoth desires that Osiris live and I may help to effect this much of his will. In the meantime, I shall be thinking."

"That is good enough."

"See how the gauntlet grows! Further than before! It is down to my thighs this time!"

"Excellent! The more of you becomes invicible, the better for us all."

"A moment. Do you seriously think the three of us can defeat Thoth, Set and the Steel General?"

"Yes."

"How?"

"The Hammer may strike again," says Anubis.

"It still exists?"

"Yes, and Osiris is its master."

"Well, granting all these things and assuming that even Vramin, who is now master in your House, may be dealt with— what of the other? What of the great shadow in the shape of horse which will pursue us till the end of our days, he who does not live in space as we know it, who cannot be destroyed, and who cannot be reasoned with when anger lies upon him?"

Anubis looks away.

"Typhon do I fear," he admits. "Ages ago I constructed a weapon—no, not a weapon—a thing—which I thought might serve to restrain him. When I tried to use it recently, he fell upon it and destroyed it. He also took my arm. . . . I admit that I have nothing but my wit to use against him. But one does not throw away an empire for fear of one individual. If only I knew the secret of his power. . . ."

"I heard him mention Skagganauk Abyss."

"There is no such place."

"I've never heard the name before. You have?"

"Legend, fancy, fiction."

"And what do these things tell of it?"

"We waste time discussing nonsense."

"If you wish my assistance, you will answer me. See, the gauntlet now reaches to my knees."

"Skagganauk Abyss, sometimes called the chasm in the sky," says Anubis, "is the place where it is said that all things stop and nothing exits."

"There are many very empty spaces in the universe."

"But the Abyss is said to be empty of space, also. It is a bottomless hole that is not a hole. It is a gap in the fabric of space itself. It is nothing. It is the theoretical hub of the universe. It is the big exit leading nowhere, under, over, beyond, out of it all. That's Skagganauk Abyss."

"Typhon does seem to possess these qualities himself, does he not?"

"Yes, he does; I'll admit that. But it answers nothing. Curse the mating of Set and Isis! They have begotten a brute and a monster!"

"You can hardly talk, Anubis. Was Typhon always as he is now? How could the Witch be delivered of such a one?"

"I do not know. He is older than I. That whole family is shrouded in mystery and paradox. —Let us be off to the House of Life!"

Madrak nods his head.

"Show me the way, Anubis."

Night Becomes Horus

He walks in the places of power and none know his name. But if each among the creatures that pass were to be asked, they would say that they had heard something of him. For he is a god. His power is almost beyond measure. He has been defeated, however. The Prince Who Was A Thousand, his brother, worked his undoing to preserve his own life and the order of life which he represents.

Now, Horus turns up an avenue, well lighted, where the various species cavort. Power and the night are around him.

He has come to this particular street on this particular world for a reason: He is invariably undecided. He needs opinions. He loves oracles.

He seeks advice.

Darkness in the sky, bright lights along the thoroughfare. He passes places and people of entertainment.

A man moves to bar his way. He seeks to pass around him, stepping into the street. The man follows and seizes his arm.

Horus blows his breath upon him and it comes down with

the force of a hurricane. The man is swept away and Horus moves on.

After a time, he comes to a place of oracles. The Tarot readers and the astrologers and the numerologists and the casters of the Yi Ching beckon to the god in the red loincloth. But he passes them by.

Finally, he comes to a place where there are no people.

It is the place of the machines which predict.

At random, he selects a booth, enters.

"Yes?" inquires the booth.

"Queries," Horus replies.

"A moment."

There comes a metallic click and an inner door opens.

"Enter the cubicle."

Horus moves to enter a small room. It contains a bed, of sorts. A heavy female torso lies upon it, joined with a gleaming console. A speaker is set within the wall.

"Mount the inquiry unit," he is instructed.

Discarding his loincloth, Horus does this thing.

"The rule is that your questions will be answered for so long as you give satisfaction," he is informed. "What is it that you wish to know?"

"I have a problem: I find myself in conflict with my brother. I tried to defeat him. I failed. I cannot make up my mind as to whether I should seek him out again and renew the battle. . . ."

"Insufficient information to reply," comes the answer. "What sort of conflict? What sort of brother? What sort of man are you?"

Gruesome grow the lilacs and the rose-rows be hedges of thorn. The garden of memory is filled with frantic bouquets.

"Perhaps I have come to the wrong place. . . ."

"This may be, and it may not. Obviously, though, you do not know the rules."

"Rules?" and Horus stares up at the dull mesh of the speaker.

Dry monotone, the voice is sifted through:

"I am not a seer, nor am I a foreseer. I am an electrical-mechanical-biological votary of the god Logic. Pleasure is my price, and for it I will invoke the god for any man. To do so, however, I need a more complete question. I do not possess sufficient data to answer you at this point. So love me, and tell me more."

"I do not know where to begin," Horus begins. "My brother once ruled all things—"

"Stop! Your statement is illogical, unquantifiable—"

". . . and quite correct. My brother is Thoth, sometimes called the Prince Who Was A Thousand. One time, all of the Midworlds were his kingdom."

"My records indicate the existence of a myth concerning a Lord of Life and Death. According to the myth, he had no brothers."

"Correction. These matters are generally kept within the family. Isis had three sons, one of them by her lawful Lord, Osiris; two of them by Set the Destroyer. Unto Set she begat Typhon and Thoth. Unto Osiris she begat Horus the Avenger, myself."

"Thou art Horus?"

"You have named me."

"You wish to destroy Thoth?"

"That was my assigned task."

"You cannot do it."

"Oh."

"Please do not depart. There may be more questions you wish to ask."

"I can't think of any."

But Horus cannot depart at this moment, for the fires are upon him.

"What are you?" he finally inquires.

"I have already told you."

"Yet how have you become what you are: half woman, half machine?"

"This is the one question I may not answer, unless I am properly cued. I shall, however, attempt to comfort thee, seeing that thou art distraught."

"Thank you. You are kind."

"It is my pleasure."

"I'd say that once you were human."

"That is correct."

"Why did you cease being so?"

"I may not say, as I have said."

"May I help you in any way to effect anything which you may desire?"

"Yes."

"How?"

"I may not say."

"Do you know for a fact that Horus may not destroy Thoth?"

"This is the most valid probability, based on the knowledge of the myths which I possess."

"If you were a mortal woman, I'd be inclined to be kind to you."

"What does that mean?"

"I might love you for your terrible honesty."

"My god, my god! Thou hast saved me."

"What do you mean?"

"I have been doomed to this existence till one who is greater than men shall look upon me with love."

"I might look upon you in such a manner. Would you deem that probable?"

"No, for I am too used."

"Then you know not the god Horus."

"It is the utmost improbability."

"But I've no one else to love. So I love you."

"The god Horus loves me?"

"Yes."

"Then thou art my Prince, and thou hast come."

"I do not—"

"Bide thou a moment and other things shall occur."

"I shall abide," says Horus, standing.

The Thing
That Is the Heart

Vramin walks through the House of the Dead. Had you eyes in that place, you couldn't see a thing. It is far too dark for eyes to be of value. But Vramin can see.

He walks through an enormous room, and when he reaches a certain point within it there comes a light that is dim and orange and crowded into corners.

Then they come up out of the transparent rectangles which now appear in the floor, come up unbreathing, unblinking and horizontal, and they rest upon invisible catafalques at a height of two feet, and their garments and skins are of all colors and their bodies of all ages. Now some have wings and some have tails, and some have horns and some long talons. Some have all of these things, and some have pieces of machinery built into them and some do not.

There comes a moaning and a creaking of brittle bones, then movement.

Rustling, clicking, chafing, they sit up, they stand up.

Then all bow down before him, and one word fills the air:

"*Master.*"

He turns his green eyes upon the multitude, and from somewhere a sound of laughter comes to fall upon his ears.

Turning, turning, turning, he waves his cane.

Then there is a sudden movement and she stands by his side.

"Vramin, your new subjects pay you homage."

"Lady, how did you get in here?"

But she laughs again and does not answer his question.

"I, too, have come to honor thee: Hail Vramin! Lord of the House of the Dead!"

"You are kind, Lady."

"I am more than kind. The end draws near, and that which I desire is almost at hand."

"It was you who raised these dead?"

"Of course."

"Do you know the whereabouts of Anubis?"

"No, but I can help you find him."

"Then let us lay these dead to rest once more, and I may ask your assistance. I may also ask what it is that you desire."

"And I may tell you."

And the dead suddenly lie down and descend into their graves. The light departs.

"Do you know why Anubis fled?" he inquires.

"No, I am only just arrived here."

"He departed, pursued by your son Typhon."

And the Red Witch smiles within her veils.

"That Typhon lives pleases me beyond measure," she says. "Where is he now?"

"Presently, he is seeking the life of Osiris. It may be that he has already disposed of both the dog and the bird."

And she laughs, and her familiar leaps upon her shoulder and holds its stomach with both hands.

"How joyous a thing this would be—now! We must look upon this affair!"

"Very good," and Vramin draws a green picture-frame upon the dark air.

Isis moves to his side and takes his hand in hers.

Suddenly there is a picture within the frame, and it moves.

It is the picture of a dark horse shadow, alone, moving upon a wall.

"This is of no help to us," says Vramin.

"No, but it is good to look upon my son once again, my son who contains the Abyss of Skagganauk within him. Where may his brother be?"

"With his father, as they have gone to fight the Nameless once again."

And Isis drops her eyes and the picture wavers.

"I would look upon this thing," she finally says.

"Before this, I would locate Anubis and Osiris, if they still live—and Madrak."

"Very well."

And within its emerald frame, the picture slowly takes form.

Upon This Bank
and Shoal

Standing there, he observes the Thing That Cried In The Night.

It cries no longer.

Freed, it leans toward him, a tower of smoke, a beard without a chin. . . .

Raising the star wand, he traces a pattern of fires across its middle.

It continues to advance.

The fires run the gamut of the spectrum, vanish.

It begins to vibrate, and his hands adjust the wand.

It coils about him, then draws back.

Standing there, above the clouds and all, he unleashes lightnings upon it.

An humming sound occurs.

The star wand vibrates within his hand, emits a whining note, grows brighter.

The Thing falls back. Set strides across the sky, attacking it.

It drops, falls, retreats, toward the surface of the world.

Pursuing, Set stands upon a mountaintop. Somewhere, above the moon, the Prince and the General follow.

Set laughs, and the heat of an exploding sun plays along the creature's length.

But then it turns and strikes, and Set retreats across the continent, mushrooms of smoke rising in his wake.

Storms shake their curly heads. Ball lightning rolls across the sky. The perpetual twilight is brightened by a tongue of flame which falls upon his pursuer.

It advances, however, and mountains fall where it passes. Far below, the ground trembles, and the shoes upon his feet track thunderprints where Set passes, turns, turns again.

The rains pour down, the clouds thicken. Flame-tipped funnels appear below.

The creature comes on, striking, and its path is incandescent, then gray, then incandescent.

The wand rings like a bell, and the seas outleap their bounds.

The creature is assailed by all the elements, yet still it advances.

Set snarls, and the rocks grind together and the winds tear the tent of the sky down the middle, flap it, rejoin its halves.

The creature cries once more, and Set, with one foot upon the sea, smiles within his glove and delivers whirlwinds and concussions.

Yet it advances, and the air grows cold.

The typhoon rises beneath Set's hand, and the lightnings descend without letup. The ground is broken, sinks within itself.

Set and the creature strike simultaneously, and the continent is destroyed beneath them.

The oceans begin to boil, and an aurora borealis of all colors covers the entire sky.

Then three needles of white light pass through the creature, and it retreats toward the equator.

Set follows; chaos follows Set.

Thunders above the equator, and the lash, lash, lash of the star wand through the sky. . . .

Smoke the color of grass fills the middle air. Destiny's lackey, Time, repaints a backdrop behind it.

There is a cry, and again a chiming, as of a bell, as the chains of the sea are broken and the waters rise up, swaying like the pillars of Pompeii on that day, that day when they were broken, inundated; and the heat, the heat of the boiling oceans rises with them; and now the air is dense and unbreathable. Employing temporal fugue. Set crucifies the creature upon the smoldering sky, and still it cries out and lashes at him, draws back. The armor of Set is unbreached, mundane though it is, for the Thing That Cries has not touched upon him. Now Set unleashes beads of blaze that are like unto a Guy Fawkes display. The creature erupts at nineteen points, collapses upon itself. Then comes a mighty roaring, and the lightnings lance once more. The Thing That Cries In The Night becomes a bowling ball, an eight ball. It wails then to break the eardrum, and Set clutches at his head, but continues to bathe the creature in the light of his wand.

Then the screaming comes from the wand itself. A pink blade of fire descends upon the creature.

It becomes an old man with a long beard, miles high, suddenly.

It raises one hand, and there is light all about Set.

But he raises his wand and darkness devours the light, and a green trident forks forth to strike the creature upon its breast.

Falling, it becomes a sphinx, and he shatters its face with ultrasonics.

Collapsing, it becomes a satyr, and he castrates it with silver pliers.

Then it rears, wounded, to a three-mile height, cobra of black smoke, and Set knows that the moment is at hand.

He raises the star wand and makes an adjustment.

Intermezzo

Armies clash in the fog on the planet D'donori, and the golinda mate on the graves of the slain; when the crown is torn from Dilwit's head, he will be without a scalp; again, Brotz, Purtz and Dulp are blinded by their neighbors; on the world Waldik there is wailing and darkness; out of the ruins of Blis, life comes forth once again; Marachek is dead, dead, dead: color it dust; the Schism has begun on Interludici, and also the evening rains, with a purported vision of the Sacred Shoes by a monk named Bros, who may have been drug-crazed; a mad, mad wind blows beneath the sea in the Place of the Heart's Desire, and a green saurian who lives there frolics in the autumn mist, constellations of bright-bellied fishes wheeling everywhere.

Cane, Pendant,
Chariot and Away

His arm is around her waist, and together they watch the pictures that form within the frame, there in the House of the Dead. They watch Osiris, as he sails across the sky on his black crossbow, upon which is mounted a thing that can smash a sun. He rides alone, and the yellow eyes never blink within that face which cannot know expression. They watch the dark cockleshell which contains Anubis, Madrak and an empty glove which holds power.

Vramin traces two lines with the tip of his cane, extending the courses of the vessels. The picture changes to the place where the lines intersect. There lies the twilight world, and its surface undergoes upheavals as they watch.

"How is it that they could know the place?" asks Isis.

"I do not know— Unless . . . Osiris! He found a note. I watched his expression as he read it."

"And . . . ?"

"Horus. Horus must have left him the note—telling him the place."

"How could Horus know it?"

"He fought with Thoth—probably within Thoth's own mind, and Horus can look into a man's head, know what he is thinking. Sometime during that encounter, he must have stolen this knowledge from the Prince, who is normally proof against such skills. —Yes, at some time he must have let down his guard for an instant. He must be warned!"

"Perhaps Typhon will yet provide for his safety."

"Where is Typhon now?"

They regard the frame, and all pictures flee.

Black, black, black. There is nothing.

"It is as though Typhon does not exist," says Vramin.

"No," says Isis. "You look upon Skagganauk the Abyss. Typhon has withdrawn from the universe, to seek his own way along the undersides of space as men know it. It may be that he, too, has found whatever note Horus left."

"That is not sufficient insurance for the Prince. The whole project may miscarry—unless we can reach him."

"Then go to him quickly!"

"I cannot."

"One of your famous gateways . . ."

"They only function within the Midworlds. I draw my power from the tides. I cannot operate beyond. Lady, how did you come here?"

"In my chariot."

"Of the Ten Invisible Powers?"

"Yes."

"Then let us use it."

"I fear— Listen, Mage. You must understand. I am a woman and I love my son, but I also love my life. I am afraid. I fear the place of that conflict. Do not think the less of me if I refuse to accompany you. You may take my chariot and you may ride in it, but you must keep your own company."

"I think not the less of you, Lady—"

"Then take this pendant. It controls the Ten Powers that drive the chariot, and it will give you additional strengths."

"Will it function beyond the Midworlds?"

"Yes," and she slides into his arms, and for a moment his green beard tickles her neck while her familiar gnashes its tiny teeth and knots its tail, twice.

Then she conducts him to her chariot on the roof of the House of the Dead, and he mounts it, holds high the pendant in his right hand, becomes for a moment part of a cleverly contrived tableau within a red glass bottle, is then a distant twinkle in the heavens Isis watches.

Shuddering, she retreats to the places of the dead, to dwell again upon the one whom she fears to face, who is even now battling the Nameless.

Vramin stares ahead with eyes of jade. Points of yellow light dance within them.

To the Place of Fire

Behind Vramin's eyes is the vision distilled. . . .

There stands the Prince, downward staring. The surface of the world's afire. On the prow of the Prince's boat stands the beast whose body is armor, whose rider sits unmoving, gleaming, also facing the place of conflict. The crossbow approaches. The cockleshell swings forward. The Hammer is cocked, snaps forward. Then, rag-tail ablaze, the comet comes forth, glowing, brightening as it races onward.

Somewhere, a banjo is plucked as Bronze rears and the head of the General swivels over his left shoulder to face the intruder. His left hand jerks toward him and Bronze continues to rear, up onto his hindmost legs and then springs away from the Prince's vessel. Three strides only are taken. Mount and rider vanish. There comes a haziness, a crinkling, and the stars dance in that corner of the sky as though they were reflections within an agitated pool. The comet is caught up in this wind that is Change, becomes two-dimensional, is gone. Pieces of the broken crossbow continue on along the path the vessel had followed when whole. The cockleshell heads toward the surface of the world, vanishes amid the smoke and the dust, the flames. For a long while, the entire tableau is a still life. Then the cockleshell streaks away. It now contains three occupants.

Vramin tightens his hand upon the piece of bloody light, and the Chariot of Ten turns to pursue.

The conflict rages upon the surface of the planet. The globe seems a liquid and boiling thing, changing shape, spurting forth fiery fountains. There comes a series of enormous blazes and a mighty shattering. The world comes apart. There is brightness, mighty, mighty, and dust, confusion: Fragmentation.

Behind the jade eyes of Vramin, within which dance the yellow lights, there is this vision.

The Abyss

Hands clasped behind his back, the Prince Who Was A Thousand considers the destruction of the world.

The broken body of the world, its members splintered and crushed, rotates beneath him, flattening, elongating, burning, burning, burning.

Now he watches through an instrument as he orbits the ruin, an instrument like a pink lorgnette with antennae. Occasionally, there is a click and the antennae twitch. He lowers it, raises it again, several times. Finally, he puts it aside.

"What is it that you see, my brother?"

He turns his head, and the dark horse shadow is at his side.

"I see a living point of light, caught up in that mass down there," he says. "Twisted, shrunken, weakly pulsing, but still alive. Still living . . ."

"Then our father has failed."

"I fear so."

"This thing must not be."

And Typhon is gone.

* * *

Now, as Vramin pursues the cockle of Anubis, he sees the thing for which there is no understanding.

Upon the blasted heap of elements that was a world there comes now a dark spot. It grows, amidst the light, the dust, the confusion, grows until its outline becomes discernible:

It is a dark horse shadow that has fallen upon the rubble.

It continues to grow until it achieves the size of a continent.

Rearing, the dark horse is rampant over all. It swells, it expands, it lengthens, until the wreckage of the entire planet is contained within it.

Then it is framed in flame.

Nothing lies within the blazing silhouette. Nothing whatsoever.

Then the flames subside and the shadow shrinks, retreating, retreating, running down a long, absolutely empty corridor.

Then there is nothing.

It is as if the world had never existed. It is gone, finished, kaput, and the Nameless Thing That Cries In The Night along with it. And now, Typhon, too, is gone.

A line comes into Vramin's head: "Die Luft ist kuhl und es dunkelt, und ruhig fliesst der Rhein." He does not recall the source, but knows the feeling.

Bloodbolt held on high, he pursues the god of death.

Ship of Fools

Awakening, slowly, manacled spread-eagle fashion to a steel table, bright lights stabbing down through his yellow eyes like electric needles within his brain, Set groans softly and tests the strength of his bonds.

His armor is gone, that pale glow in the corner might be the star wand, his shoes that walk upon everything are not to be seen.

"Hello, Destroyer," says the wearer of the glove. "You are fortunate to have survived the encounter."

"Madrak . . . ?" he asks.

"Yes."

"I can't see you. Those lights. . . ."

"I'm standing behind you, and those lights are only for purposes of preventing your use of temporal fugue to depart this vessel before we are ready to permit it."

"I do not understand."

"The battle waxeth furious below. I am watching it through

181

a port now. It looks as if you have the upper hand. In a moment, the Hammer That Smashes Suns will strike again, and you will of course escape it as you did the last time—by means of the fugue. That is why we were able to pick you up a few moments ago, just as Anubis did in days long gone by. The fact that you did appear testifies to what will happen shortly. There! Osiris strikes, and the Hammer begins its descent— Anubis! Something is wrong! There is some sort of change occurring! The Hammer is . . . is . . . gone. . . ."

"Yes, I see it now," comes the familiar bark. "And Osiris, too, has gone away. The Steel General—he it was."

"What shall we do now?"

"Nothing. Nothing whatsoever. This turn is even better than we had hoped. Set's occurrence recently by means of the fugue testifies that some cataclysmic event will still shortly occur.—Does it not, Set?"

"Yes."

"Your final clash will doubtless destroy the world."

"Probably. I didn't stay to watch."

"Yes, there it goes," says Madrak.

"Wonderful! Now we have Set, Osiris has been disposed of, and the Steel General is no longer available to pursue us. We have Thoth precisely where we want him. Hail, Madrak, new Lord of the House of Life!"

"Thank you, Anubis. I didn't think it could be that easily accomplished—but what of the Nameless?"

"Surely it must have fallen this time. What of it, Set?"

"I don't know. I struck it with the full force of the wand."

"Then everything is tied up neatly. Now hear me, Set. We wish you no ill, nor will we harm your son Thoth. We rescued you when we could have left you to rot—"

"Then why have you secured me thus?"

"Because I know your temper and your power, and I wished to reason with you before freeing you. You might not have granted me sufficient opportunity, so I insured it myself. I wish to deal with Thoth through you—"

"Lord!" cries Madrak. "Observe the ruined world! There comes over it a monstrous shadow!"

"It is Typhon!"

"Yes. What can he be doing?"

"What do you know of this, Set?"

"It means that I failed, and that somewhere amid the ruins a Nameless Thing still cries in the night. Typhon is completing the job."

"There is fire, master, and—I cannot look upon the emptiness which occurs—"

"Skagganauk Abyss!"

"Yes," says Set. "Typhon *is* Skagganauk Abyss. He evicts the Nameless from the universe."

"What was the Nameless?"

"A god," says Set, "an old god, I'm sure, with nothing left to be divine about any more."

"I do not understand. . . ." says Madrak.

"He jests. But what of Typhon? How shall we deal with him?"

"You may not have to," says Set. "What he has done has probably resulted in his own exile from the universe."

"Then we have won, Anubis! We have won! Typhon was the only thing you feared, was he not?"

"Yes. Now the Midworlds lie forever within my hands."

"And mine, don't forget!"

"Of course not. So tell me, Set—You see the ways the stars are drifting— Will you join with us? You will become the right hand of Anubis. Your son can be a Regent. He may name his own job, for I do not undervalue his wisdom. What say you?"

"I must think of this thing, Anubis."

"To be sure. Take your time. Realize, however, that I am now invincible."

"And you realize that I have defeated God in battle."

"It could not have been God," says Madrak, "or He would not have been defeated!"

"No," says Set. "You saw Him at the end. You witnessed His power. And even now, He is not dead, only in exile."

Madrak lowers his head, covers his face with his hands. "I do not believe you! I cannot. . . ."

"But it is true, and you have been party to this thing, oh recreant priest, blasphemer, apostate!"

"Silence, Set!" cries Anubis. "Don't listen to him, Madrak. He sees your weakness, as he sees the weaknesses of all things he encounters. He seeks to draw you onto a battlefield of another sort, one where you struggle against yourself, to be beaten by the guilt he has contrived for you. Ignore him!"

"But what if he speaks the truth? I stood by and did nothing—even profited by—"

"Indeed you did," says Set. "The guilt is mainly mine, but I bear it with pride. You were party to the action, however. You stood by and watched, thinking of the profit that would come to you, while He whom you served was beaten to His knees—"

Anubis strikes him a terrible blow that rips the flesh of his cheek.

"I take it that you have made up your mind, and this is your answer: to try to turn Madrak against me. It will not work. He is not so gullible as you think—are you, Dad?"

Madrak does not answer, but continues to stare out the port.

Set struggles against his bonds but cannot loose them.

"Anubis! We are pursued!"

Anubis departs Set's side, vanishing into darkness. The lights continue to stab downward.

"It is the Chariot of Ten," Anubis says.

"Of the Lady Isis?" Madrak inquires. "Why should she follow us?"

"Because Set was once her beloved. Perhaps he still is. Eh, Set? What's the story?"

But Set does not reply.

"Whatever," says Madrak, "it draws near. How strong is the Red Witch? Will she give us trouble?"

"She was not so strong but that she feared her old Lord, Osiris, avoiding him for many centuries—and I am certainly as strong as Osiris. We will not be beaten by a woman—not when we have come this far."

Madrak bows his head, mumbling, and begins to beat upon his breast.

"Stop that! You're being ridiculous!"

But Set laughs, and Anubis turns upon him with a snarl.

"I'll tear your heart out for that!"

But Set raises his bleeding left hand which he has just torn free and holds it before his body.

"Try it, dog! Your one hand against mine! Your staff and any other weapon you have against the left hand of Set! Come closer!" and his eyes glow like twin suns and Anubis falls back beyond his grasp.

The lights continue to dazzle and spin.

"Kill him, Madrak!" cries Anubis. "He is of no further use to us! You wear the gauntlet of power! He cannot stand against it!"

But Madrak does not reply; instead, "Forgive me, Whatever You Are or Were, wherever You May or May Not Be, for omissions and commissions in which I indulged or did not indulge, as the case may be, in this matter which has just come to pass," he says, still beating his breast. "And in the event that—"

"Then give me the glove!" cries Anubis. "Quickly!"

But Madrak continues, unhearing.

A shudder runs through the cockleshell, and magicians and poets being very good at that sort of thing, a doorway which had been doubly sealed springs open and Vramin enters.

He waves his cane and smiles.

"How do? How do?"

"Take him, Madrak!" cries Anubis.

But Vramin advances and Madrak stares out the window, mumbling.

Then Anubis raises his staff before him.

"Angel of the Seventh Station, and fallen, depart!" says Anubis.

"You use my old title," says Vramin. "I am now Angel of the House of the Dead."

"You lie."

"No. By appointment of the Prince do I now occupy your former position."

With a great wrenching movement, Set frees his right hand.

Vramin dangles Isis' pendant before him, and Anubis backs away.

"Madrak, I bid you destroy this one!" he cries out.

"Vramin?" says Madrak. "Oh no, not Vramin. He is good. He is my friend."

Set frees his right ankle.

"Madrak, if you will not destroy Vramin, then hold Set!"

"'Thou Who might be our Father Who perhaps may be in Heaven . . .'" Madrak intones.

Then Anubis snarls and points his staff like a bazooka at Vramin.

"Come no farther," he announces.

But Vramin advances another step.

A blaze of light falls upon him, but the red beams from the pendant cancel it out.

"Too late, dog," he says.

Anubis circles, draws near the port where Madrak stands.

Set frees his left ankle, rubs it, stands.

"You are dead," says Set, and moves forward.

But at this moment, Anubis falls to the knife of Madrek, which enters his neck above the collarbone.

"I meant no harm," says Madrak, "and this is to pay in part for my guilt. The dog led me astray. I repent. I make you a gift of his life."

"Thou fool!" says Vramin. "I wanted him prisoner."

Madrak begins to weep.

Anubis bleeds in red spurts upon the deck of the cockle-shell.

Set lowers his head slowly and rubs his eyes.

"What shall we do now?" asks Vramin.

"'. . . Hallowed by Thy name, if a name Thou hast and any desire to see it hallowed. . . .'" says Madrak.

Set does not answer, having closed his eyes and fallen into a sleep that will last for many days.

Femina Ex Machina

And she lies there big with child within the chassis of the machine. A wall of the cubicle has drawn back. The wires have fallen away from her head and her spine, disconnecting the icy logic, the frigid memory banks, the sex-comp compulsions, the nutrient tubes. She is deprogramed.

"Prince Horus . . ."

"Megra. Rest easy."

". . . You have broken the enchantment."

"Who did this terrible thing to you?"

"The Witch of the Loggia."

"Mother! Her ways have always been wild, Megra. I am sorry." He places his hand upon her. "Why did she do this thing?"

"She told me that a thing of which I was unaware—that I am to bear Set's child—is the reason—"

"Set!" and Horus' fingerprints are imbedded in the metal table. "Set. —Did he take you by force?"

"Not exactly."

"Set . . . What are your feelings toward him now?"

"I hate him."

"That will be sufficient."

"He cares nothing for life. . . ."

"I know. I shall not ask you of him again. You will come away with me to the House of Life, Megra of Kalgan, and dwell with me there forever."

"But, Horus, I fear that I must be delivered here. I am too weak to go far, and my time is near."

"Then so be it. We shall abide for a time within this place."

And she clasps her hands upon her belly and closes her cobalt eyes. The glow of the machine causes her cheeks to blaze.

Horus sits by her side.

Soon she cries out.

The Marriage of Heaven and Hell

The Citadel of Marachek, empty, not empty, empty again. Why? Listen. . . .

Set stands his ground, facing the monster, and it lunges toward him.

For a long while they wrestle, there in the courtyard.

Then Set breaks its back, and it lies a groaning.

His eyes blaze like suns, and he turns them once again to the place where he had been headed.

Then Thoth, his son, his father, the Prince Who Was A Thousand, opens again the bottle of instant monsters and removes another seed.

Sowing it there in the dust, another menace blooms beneath his hand, then bends toward Set.

The madness that lies within Set's eyes falls upon the creature and there is more conflict.

Standing above its broken body, Set bows his head and vanishes.

But Thoth follows after him sowing monsters, and the ghosts

of Set and the monsters he fights rage through the marble memory that is wrecked and rebuilt Marachek, the oldest city.

And each time that Set destroys a creature, he turns his eyes once again toward a place, a moment, where he had battled the Nameless and destroyed a world and where the dark horse shadow his son rears and blazes; and heeding the beck of annihilation he moves toward that place, that moment. But Thoth follows, distracting him with monsters.

This is because Set is destruction, and he will destroy himself if there is nothing else that is suitable at hand or somewhere in sight, in time or in space. But the Prince is wise and realizes this. This is why he follows after his father on his temporal journey toward the altar of annihilation, after his awakening from the trance of battle against the Thing That Cries In The Night. For Thoth knows that if he can distract him long enough from his pilgrimage, new things will arise toward which Set's hand may be turned. This is because such things always arise.

But not they move through time, filling perhaps all of time, considered from this moment of it—the wise Prince and his deadly father/son—skirting always the Abyss that is Skagganauk, son, brother and grandson.

This is why the ghosts of Set and the monsters he fights rage through the marble memory that is wrecked and rebuilt Marachek, the oldest city.

Witch Dream

She sleeps, in the House of the Dead, in a deep, dark, buried crypt, and consciousness is a snowflake, melting, gone now. But the motorcycle that is Time backfires as it races by, and there, within the remembered mirror, lie the last days' battles: Osiris dead, and gone away Set. And there is the green laughter of Vramin; Vramin, mad and a poet, too. Hardly fit Lord for the Witch of the Loggia. Better not to set an alarm. Sleep away an age, then see what Thoth hath wrought. Here, amid the mummy-dust and the burned-out tapers, here in the bottommost cellar of the House of the Dead, where none have names nor seek them, and where none will be sought; here: Sleep. Sleep, and let the Middle Worlds go by, ignorant of the Red Lady who is Lust, Cruelty, Wisdom and mother and mistress of invention and violent beauty.

The creatures of light and darkness dance on the guillotine's lip, and Isis fears the poet. The creatures of light and darkness don and discard the garments of man, machine and god; and Isis loves the dance. The creatures of light and darkness are born in great numbers, die in an instant, may rise again, may not rise again; and Isis approves of the garments.

Dreaming these dreams and fearful, her familiar presses close against her, a little thing that cries in the night.

Wheels turning, the motorcycle's roar grows steady, which, too, is a form of silence.

Angel of
the House of Life

(They come in the middle of the night, walking. There are three of them, together moving down places of belief and disbelief. They pass the places of entertainment for many species, coming at last to the well-lighted Avenue of the Oracles and moving along it, passing by astrologers, numerologists, Tarot readers and casters of the Yi Ching.

Now, as they advance, they move from light to lesser light, from dimness and dankness to twilight and squalor. The sky hangs clear above them and the stars shine down. The street grows more narrow, the buildings lean toward them; the gutters are filled with refuse; children with sunken eyes stare at them, nearly weightless within the circles of their mothers' arms.

They step over the rubbish; they walk through it. And none dare accost these three. Strength hangs about them like an odor and purpose gives them a certain distinction.

Their bearing is graceful and their cloaks are rich. They walk where the cats scramble and the bottles are broken, and it is as though these things were not.

Above them, there is a blaze in the heavens, as the light from a world that Set destroyed finally reaches this one, coming like a new star in the sky and splashing them with colors red through blue.

The wind is cold but they do not heed it. The word for copulation, in ninety-four languages, is scrawled upon one wall, but they do not notice.

It is only when they come to a dilapidated machine that they pause before an obscene drawing upon its doorway.)

First

This is the place.

Second

Then let us enter.

Third

Yes.

(The first touches the door with his silver-headed cane and it swings open.

He enters, and the others follow.

They pass along a corridor, and he touches another door.

It, too, opens before them, and they pause once more.)

Horus

You!

(The one whose eyes flash green within the shadows nods.)

Why are you here?

195

The man who wears the iron ring
To tell you that your father is dead.

Horus
Who are you?

The man who wears the iron ring
You knew me as the Steel General. I slew Osiris and was broken myself. The Prince collected me and I wear the flesh once more, for a time. I come to tell you that this thing is so, and to say to your face that it was not a deed of stealth or malice, but an open act of combat in time of war.

Horus
You are a man of truth. Among all creatures, I do not doubt your word. And I seek no satisfaction if the deed was fair and in time of war.
And how went the war?

Fat man, all in black
Whose one eye is a gray wheel, turning
The Prince holds the Middle Worlds once more.

Vramin
And we are his emissaries, come to request your return to the House of Life, that you may rule there now in your father's stead, as Angel of that place.

Horus
I see. What of Set?

Vramin
He is gone away. None knows where.

Horus

This likes me. More than a little. Yes, I suppose I'll return.

MADRAK *(dropping to one knee beside Megra of Kalgan.*
What child is this?

Horus

My son.

Madrak

The son of Horus. Have you a name for him?

Horus

Not yet.

Madrak

Congratulations.

General

Yes.

Vramin

Many.

Horus

Thank you.

Vramin

I give him the pendant of Isis, which is a thing of power. I know she would like her grandson to have it.

Horus

Thank you.

General

I give him a ring that is a piece of my first body, which served me well. It has always reminded me of humanity, in times of need.

Horus

Thank you.

Madrak

I give him my staff, that it may comfort him. For there is an ancient tradition that staves have a way of doing that. I don't know why.

Horus

Thank you.

Madrak

I must depart now and begin my pilgrimage of repentance. Hail, Angel of the House of Life!

Horus

A good journey to you, Madrak.
(Madrak departs.)

General

There is a revolution I must encourage. I go to find my horse. Hail, Angel of the House of Life!

Horus

A good revolution to you, General.
(The General departs.)

Vramin

And I go to the House of the Dead, where I now rule. Hail, Angel of the House of Life! The Prince will contact you one day from Marachek. And the other Angels of the other Stations will assemble to pay you honor.

Horus

A fine poetry and a good madness to you, Vramin.

Vramin

Thank you, and I guess that's about all there is to be said.

Horus

So it would seem.

(Vramin raises his cane and a poem falls and blazes upon the floor.

Horus lowers his eyes to read it, and when he looks up again the green man is gone.

As the poem fades, the Angel of the House of Life knows that it was true but forgets the words, which is as it should be.)